D0929005

Items should be return
shown below. Items not
borrower
to

THE SUMMERHOUSE

By the same author:

A Time Outworn
A Peacock Cry
Antiquities
An Idle Woman
A Friend of Don Juan
Very Like A Whale

THE SUMMERHOUSE

Val Mulkerns

Third edition

Tara
press

The Summerhouse, Third Edition, 2013
Published by
Tara Press, New York, Dublin

Trade and order inquiries to:
editor@tarapress.net
www.tarapress.net

First published 1984
by John Murray (Publishers) Ltd
50 Albemarle Street, London W1X 4BD
www.johnmurray.co.uk

ISBN: 978-0-9545620-3-8

Cover and interior design - www.Cyberscribe.ie
Cover Image: www.etsy.com/shop/TanyDiDesignStudio

For Sean O'Faoláin

ABOUT THE AUTHOR

Val Mulkerns is an Irish writer and member of Aosdána. Her first novel, *A Time Outworn*, was released to critical acclaim in Ireland in 1951. She later worked as a journalist and columnist and is often heard on the radio. She is the author of four novels, three collections of short stories, two children's books and many published essays and critical writings. She lives in Dublin, Ireland.

For more information please see:
www.valmulkerns.com

The harvest is past,
the summer is ended,
and we are not saved.

JEREMIAH (8:20)

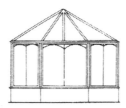

I thought of Miss Havisham when we walked into the old kitchen in Ferrycarrig the day Hanny died in Cork. She had only been five weeks away, having been found unconscious with a broken hip one April morning up in the garden. A spell of unseasonably hot weather had followed and Hanny had not been reckoning on going anywhere. She had not gone anywhere for three or four years, and the last breakfast she'd prepared had a coating of mould all over it on the table. What had been a saucer of milk on the floor looked alive under its hairy growth, and some enterprising spider had spun a trap for flies over the decayed jam in a silver dish. Half a slice of bread was green on a blue plate and there seemed to be over all the other signs of breakfast – the silver teapot, the strange-looking half-melted butter, the solidified milk – an invisible skein of decay.

Dust covered the silent old cluttered flagged kitchen, of which all my memories were noisy ones – laughter, conversation, voices raised in argument. This was a house to which scattered members of a large family had come home most summers, bringing a new wife or child to be inspected, slipping for a couple of weeks or months even into a way of living that hadn't changed much in fifty years. The summer I married Martin I realised exactly how dotty a handsome, perfectly normal-looking old lady could be, and I realised something stranger. That family did not spend months together every year because they liked one another.

One evening after supper I was introduced to Mama, so called by the grown men and women who were Martin's uncles and aunts. Before this I had only heard Mama talked about. I was told she was not well enough to meet a new granddaughter-in-law but how glad she would be to meet me when at last they could wheel her down. She looked a little formidable, with a high-necked blouse, white hair arranged like a bird's nest over some sort of frame, fine black and slightly hostile eyes under bushy eyebrows. She was not delighted to see me. She looked back annoyed at the daughter who was in charge of her wheelchair.

'I won't see Alex's wife, you know that. Don't bring me near her.'

'This is not Alex's wife, Mama, how could she be? You know Alex's wife died during the war. This is Ruth, Martin's wife. Margaret's son Martin's wife – won't you say hello to her?'

'Margaret had no sons, only two crimped and spoiled lassies, that would annoy the life and soul out of you.'

'They were Nora's girls, Mama. Margaret had two sons.'

I excused myself suddenly at this point and rushed to find Martin. 'Come up with me or I can't face her. She keeps mixing me up with somebody else.'

'That would be Alex's wife, her King Charles's head. The old girl is nutty as a fruit cake, but you have to meet her some time and it might as well be now before she takes to her bed for the last time. All right, I'll go up with you. I was keeping out of the way because for some reason she's not too keen on me either at present.'

This time the old lady in the bay window held out a claw hand. Evening light from the harbour was all around her, adding to her good looks.

'How do you do, Ruth?' The old voice was civil now but automatic, like a child's repeating a lesson.

'I'm very well thank you, Grandmother, and delighted to meet you. I'm so glad you're better.'

'Hello Gran.' Martin bent casually and kissed the old face which recoiled as from a blow.

'Who are you, young man?'

'Come on, Mother,' Eleanor behind the chair said briskly, 'You know perfectly well that Martin had a patch worn up the centre of the stairs bringing you sprats he caught when he was little. Once he tripped with a two pound jam-jar full of seawater and it took us weeks to dry out the carpet.' Martin laughed and we all followed.

'I'll catch you something better for your lunch tomorrow, Gran,' he promised, 'I'm taking Ruth out fishing in the morning. Jer Power is lending us the boat for the last day.'

'Where are you going away to?' rapped the old woman. 'Why can't you both stay here?'

'Work, Gran. Ruth and I have to go back to work in Dublin. The holidays are over.'

'The honeymoon,' Eleanor reminded her mother again. 'Ruth and Martin have just got married. We told you – you had a piece of the cake.'

'I will not see Alex's wife,' the old woman said again and Martin cast up his eyes in defeat, 'she's beneath him in brains and breeding with an outlandish name I can never remember.'

'She had', said Hanny from the corner where she was playing patience as usual, 'a perfectly ordinary name for an English girl, Mama. She was called Janet – in fact it's a Scots name too.'

'Moreover she's been dead for donkeys' years,'

Eleanor snapped. She was the best looking and shortest tempered of the aunts. 'Won't you say goodnight to Ruth now?'

The impassive old face turned away and the claw hand I had touched earlier waved to somebody taking an evening stroll below in the street. Martin motioned me away and Eleanor smiled a wordless goodbye to both of us over her mother's head. She was the one of that family who interested me most, but it was several years before I got to know her well.

We had a couple of sons by then and Martin used to urge me down here with them as soon as the school where I taught broke up for the summer months. He got away from town himself whenever he could, but for quite a lot of the time I was thrown on Eleanor for company. Each July and August she got a locum tenens to take over her practice in Cork, and she came down here with her family. We went walking most warm evenings after supper, leaving Margaret, my mother-in-law, and Hanny to keep an eye on young and old. Eleanor's husband was there too but seldom found favour with anybody in that house, including his wife. Meeting him on the stairs one hot evening when we were on our way out, I realised for the first time how people who had once cared for one another enough to marry could become strangers, and it made me a little frantic.

'We're off for a walk, Con – like to come with us?'
I invited without thinking, and I could feel Eleanor
stiffen beside me. She need not have worried. Con
knew the rules. He shook his neat grey head, smiled,
stood ironically to attention to let us pass on the stairs,
and said he would see us later. He had the remains of
trim military good looks, and an air like Eleanor's of
belonging to a world outside that didn't exist any more.
Unlike Eleanor, he accepted his lowered status with
humility; he still had a lot to learn about so many things,
his humorous expression seemed to say. Learning might
even be enjoyable.

Eleanor, unteachable, linked her skinny arm
through mine and forced the pace until we had left
the old town behind in its cradle of reflected light. You
could see the harbour at the end of two dozen or more
laneways in that town, some arched from medieval
times, some open, all smelling of seaweed and doubtful
drains and (I fancied) brandy which sailors had been
bartering these hundreds of years for homely items like
eggs or cheese or new potatoes or cartwheels of new
bread from the town's ovens. When I said something
of this to Eleanor she shrugged, never interested in
anything that was available to be enjoyed, except my
children, and King's Amusements out at the end of the
promenade. She was not, obviously, heading for King's
tonight to spend an hour trying to throw rubber rings

over hideous ornaments which she liked to leave in gardens on the way home if by any chance she won any. Winning was important to Eleanor. Her long legs forced the pace now along a sandy track that led for a mile or so away from the coast and then back to a rocky headland where a couple of cottages had fallen into ruins among the tough sea grasses. From here you could see the town toylike with its sunset spires, its encircling black walls, its golden rooftops. It might even have seemed like a big important town to somebody growing up on this headland. I said this idly to Eleanor and she laughed so that I saw the only ugly thing about her, the jumbled dark teeth which might have been pretty and sharp like a cat's when she was a girl.

'That,' she said, pointing to the nearest fallen cottage, 'that is the O'Connor family mansion. Isn't it an imposing ruin in the twilight? That's where he grew up, running wild in tattered britches like his mad mother and his raft of fatherless brothers and sisters.'

'Fatherless?' I said.

'The old lad was lost at sea (they said) before Con was born,' Eleanor said contemptuously. 'Probably found a better part of the world to live in and never came home again. "Lost at sea", that's what they always said, but I never believed it. Romantic eyewash.'

'Why are you telling me this?' I liked Con as much as I liked her and was embarrassed by her malice.

'Because you're young and taken in by his grand diplomatic airs and graces. As I was. He's a nobody, a peasant. I despise him,' she said calmly, sitting down on a mound of fallen stone with a quick movement of arms encircling knees that made you once again see the glossy-braided girl behind the lined face, brown from years of living abroad. When she was happy, maybe helping to bath the boys, she could be beautiful still, but not now, and not either when she looked with contempt, as she often did, at her large ageing daughter whom she dressed in worn out garments of her own.

I didn't know what to say, so I walked away, depressed and baffled. I wished Martin were here to puzzle over this thing with me. I wished Martin were here anyhow. Eleanor was his favourite aunt. In the slightly chill wind up on the headland I stood still and tried to imagine what he would say. Remind me, no doubt, of the fact that she was the beauty of the family, spoiled from childhood because she was a credit to them, the only one of the sisters who was as clever as the boys. Her famous winning of the Exhibition in 1911 was commemorated by a gilt-framed photograph up in the drawing-room. Her MB parchment, achieved at a time when few women went in for medicine, was lightly held like a fan in her hand in the companion photograph which was blown up to the size of her parents' wedding group and also framed in gilt on the wall. She had hair frivolously curled like Sarah Bernhardt's and the mortarboard looked like a touch of fancy dress sitting on top of it. Underneath was the face of a proud beauty which she had still – a curl to the lips and a smile in the audacious eyes that were still dark and sumptuous. Suddenly she came over and laid her hand on my shoulder almost as a man might. I had a feeling she was going to apologise for what I saw as self-indulgence which was as unfair to me as to her husband. But she didn't apologise. Once again I wished for the company of Martin and wondered why I spent so long away from home in a place that suddenly seemed alien.

'It's not much after half past nine – let's go to King's,' Eleanor said suddenly. 'It's always better out the Prom end. I don't know why I brought you to this dismal place.'

It was the nearest she could come to an apology, but she knew perfectly well it wasn't the place I found depressing. I don't really remember the rest of that night apart from dozens of others. At King's there was fairground music, the clatter of the chairoplanes whirling their human cargo out under the stars, screaming with the fear for which they paid their sixpences. 'Anything that's a sufficient shock to the system can become an addiction,' Eleanor told me. 'There was a boy in this town once who went up there fifteen times in one night. He kept on going until there wasn't another penny in his pocket and he was in a fainting condition. Come to the Hoopla, will you?'

In the noisy darkness we would play Hoopla over and over again. The sound of the last train from Cork would eventually obliterate all the other sounds and then Eleanor might remember we ought to be getting home or I would voice anxiety about the babies. On the way through the buzzing crowds she would usually stop at the Wheel of Fortune and buy two tickets, then I would buy two more, and we might win a large plaster statue of the Infant of Prague or a hideous mirror for above the fireplace. The object might be carried home where it would be exclaimed over by Hanny and Margaret and Eleanor's daughter Julia and smiled indulgently at by Con. Then it would be re-parcelled and left under the stairs in case it might do somebody in the town some time for a wedding present. Sometimes, as I said, Eleanor would giggle on the way home and leave the prize outside somebody's front door and then we would amuse ourselves by speculating on the wonder, delight or impatience of the householder when the morning revealed what God had sent. Whenever we did this Eleanor would chuckle off and on all the way home and even sometimes be kind to her sad daughter or her adopted son Andrew and kiss them goodnight.

Julia was for me one of the eternal mysteries of that house. At the time I first knew her she must have been in her mid twenties, brown eyed and bun-faced and much too tall. She dropped things easily, and if asked to do two or three errands at the same time she seldom brought back more than one of them. Her clothes were shabby but elegant and didn't suit her; sometimes I imagined what she would look like in the sort of garments that would be natural for her, baggy golden brown trousers and check shirts, and I was positive she would look better in them and be happier. Once I bought her a check shirt for her birthday, but though she exclaimed over it in delight she never wore it and eventually Eleanor did, giving me a little shamefaced grin when she saw me looking at it but passing the matter off with a joke about some people never knowing what suited them: Julia that was.

Julia was not stupid although everybody behaved as though she were. She had not shone at school, as the rest of that family had. There was nothing from Julia to add to the local newspaper clippings about notable academic achievements with which the house abounded. Two or three of the more outstanding notices were framed and hanging on the dining-room wall. They were yellowed and faded by now but still remarked on by new visitors, including myself. One of the more beautiful pieces of furniture upstairs was a tall mahogany cabinet of Chippendale design, made originally for some architect long dead but always used by Mama for filing away certificates and school reports, parchments and relevant documents which the family had achieved over the years. There were at least four dozen little separate brass-handled drawers, some of them tubular for rolled parchments, and all of them doubly protected by the tall gleaming mahogany double doors. When the old lady became too dotty to carry on her self-imposed task, Margaret, Martin's mother, took over and I knew (but didn't mind although Martin and I often laughed over it) that the academic progress of the infants we had added to the family would in due course join the collection, from their first school reports onwards, if we handed them over.

Julia had been average and (her parents said) lazy. She had managed to scrape through her school exams but had not lasted long at the veterinary course in Dublin. Then she tried to train as a children's nurse but developed some mysterious illness that affected her concentration and eventually she came home, glad to accept something like the position of a servant even during holidays in the old house. I liked and trusted her but nobody else did. Her awkwardness was remarked on every time she left the room. People told stories about the more valuable things she had broken from time to time and I was advised to be careful about leaving the babies in her charge. Their grandmother, Margaret, would be delighted to mind them any time I wanted to go out and so would Hanny or Eleanor, of course. It would, in fact, quite often be Eleanor who would issue the warning, Eleanor who would always appear during the pleasant if time-consuming job of bathing the boys every morning, laying out a change of clothes with the talcum, brushes and the warm towels into which they would be lifted out of the small tub. When they were very small they would be bathed together in the one tub which we used to set up on the kitchen table, and I can see Eleanor strolling out into the green-dappled sunlight of the flagged yard with an infant wrapped in one of the rough white towels with which that house abounded. She would sit on a wicker chair to dry the small silken head with a soft towel taken from her pocket. She would sing sometimes, and on hot days lift the baby up into the sunshine to dry him out in the most natural way. I would follow her out there with the other child and we would pass the hairbrush and comb to one another, and she would sing dandling songs she said were Greek and which she learned from the nursemaids in Athens.

Sometimes a watching shadow in the kitchen window would turn out to be Julia, smiling at the sight of the babies in the sun. It was Julia who was on hand always for the less enjoyable tasks which followed, washing the bundles of clothes to spread out on the line, making up sufficient feeds in sterile bottles to last for twenty-four hours, leaving everything to hand in the dark stone-flagged larder. There was no fridge in that house and sometimes I worried over the cobwebs trailing outside the larder window, wondering how clean the floor was and if any insects might be indoors. I didn't want to offend the family by washing the stone floor myself, but when I made the slightest mention of anxiety to Julia one day I found her on her knees a while later scrubbing away, to the scolding annoyance of Hanny who had wanted a message in the town.

Hanny was the aunt who should have liked Julia best, but she couldn't abide the sight of her. She said Julia had black fingers instead of green and plants died at her touch. This was the only criticism Julia passionately resented.

I found her crying as she laid the table the day Hanny had this outburst and she told me the story as I helped her set out the places for lunch. That morning had worn away more than most over the apparently endless tasks of looking after two babies on holiday and I'd been just about to go for a swim when I caught sight of Julia through the open door. When she saw me she brushed her hand across her eyes and pretended nothing was wrong.

'You're lying Julia. Why were you crying?'

'A speck of dust that got into my eye, that's all.'

She might have been aged thirteen and I had to

laugh. 'Was it what Hanny said at breakfast? You know she didn't mean it.'

'She did, and it's not fair, or even true. The plant was half dead when she gave it to me and I tried to save it. She'd watered it too much and rotted the roots. She wouldn't believe you don't treat tropical plants like that.'

'When was this?'

'The summer I was twelve,' Julia said, threatening a fresh outburst of tears.

Mostly, however, Julia was stoical. She listened to criticism without comment, her pale bun face closed like a Buddhist's in meditation. She didn't appear to have any friends. Certainly none ever appeared around the house, and on her birthday in late June Hanny would bake her a cake but laughed the first time I went up the town for birthday candles. I tried to imagine what sort of childhood Julia had had, and once when we met by chance on the way home to lunch after I'd been out swimming I asked Con, her father. Military-looking whiskers passing through his fingers, he considered the question.

'Julia has always lived in a world of her own,' he said, 'I came nearest to getting inside it, I think, but only occasionally. She would have made a good vet, though. That would have brought her out of herself.'

'Did she have pets all around her when she was little?'

'There were cats at the Embassy in Athens, I remember,' he said slowly, 'skinny spidery cats who would climb in out of the sun's glare and sleep on the beds. Julia would carry away saucers of food from the table but her mother found food spills on the polished marble floors so that was stopped. Pets of her own? I don't think so. We moved around so much, you know. But Julia would watch a common snail for hours, or the creatures in a rock pool.'

'She was usually alone then?'

'Quite a lot, I suppose, and often in trouble. Nursemaids, apart from one called Clea, didn't get on with her very well, and I was frequently called in. She can look stubborn sometimes, as you know. But never can any child have been in more trouble for less reason. She was awkward and had none of her mother's social graces. Alas, none of her beauty either. That seems to have been what people held against her.'

'But Eleanor?' I asked doubtfully, feeling a bit treacherous, 'wasn't she delighted to have a daughter of her own?'

'She wanted sons,' he smiled, and seemed about to say something else which he changed to an invitation for a drink before lunch.

By this time I had been coming back to the house for three years and knew how extraordinary such an invitation was. In the gloom of the little pub Con touched the froth of a creamy pint with one finger and smiled again.

'No need to mention our pre-prandial drink when you get back, Ruth,' he said, 'Mama passed on a fear and distrust of the stuff right down through that family because Alex, the eldest, a midshipman in the Royal Navy was too fond of it, and lived to be a disgrace to the family. Married an English girl for which they never forgave him.'

'Janet?'

'Janet. As fair a lady with as kind a heart as you could wish to find and a laugh that would charm the birds off the hushes. But found wanting, Ruth, found wanting, like yours truly.' He smiled again the public servant's smile that had never lost its dependability. Remembering the night with Eleanor at the rocky headland I didn't know what to say, so I smiled back and shook my head.

'I'm sure you're mistaken, Con.'

It was a silly thing to say but he accepted it lightly as a way of smoothing over a silence. Then he told me about Martin's childhood here in the town, how in a way he had almost become Eleanor's son because she would never let him out of her sight. Margaret, his mother, was so often busy with school affairs, even during holidays. She had to attend conferences, make plans for next term. Martin had been a summer son of his and Eleanor's and I suddenly saw that this was why I as his wife seemed to find so much favour with them both, and why the boys were an unfailing source of delight to Eleanor.

'Have another one of those and I'll have a chaser,' Con said suddenly, and I saw him turn over a half-moon of coins in his palm with quick calculation.

'I will if I can buy them,' I said, glad I had put a pound note in the back pocket of my jeans. Eleanor was never short of money, but Con seldom seemed to have enough for needs that seemed to me quite modest. He accepted with only a slight gallant show of protest and the barman eyed me distrustfully. I was not the townsgirl Martin might have been supposed to marry and at that time in an Irish country town it was acceptable for a woman to drink but not to commit the deliberate brazenness of buying a drink.

'How are all the care, Moss?' Con enquired pacifically as the drinks were set before us, and the publican replied, 'Rightly, thank God, and your own?' He put the change in front of Con, then, without waiting for a reply however. So I was snubbed as convention required and everybody was happy. Behind the counter again, the publican lit a cigarette, picked up the 'Cork Examiner' and forgot us.

'Moss has you marked down for a bold lassie all the same,' Con smiled as he raised his Jameson. 'Why aren't you looking chastised?'

'I'm working at it.'

For the first time in three years of coming to the house, Con and I were sitting at ease together for no particular reason except a chance meeting in Main Street, and I felt happy that the snubs I had so often seen him taking with such grace from Eleanor were now dissociated for ever from me. He still talked in the soft lilting accents of this town, despite his cosmopolitan working life, and when I asked him, because it really interested me, if he ever missed it all, he shook his head.

'Not the way Eleanor does. She's lost back here, as you can see.' I couldn't see and it surprised me, but I was glad he wanted to talk on.

'Diplomatic life suited her as it never really suited yours truly. As a beautiful woman's right she had admiration and prominence in every social gathering and all the variety of company she lacks now. She did a far better job than I could ever have done at that level.'

'What exactly was your job, Con?'

'I was an Aide, but the British Ambassador in Athens of that time died suddenly and I was unexpectedly promoted. Eleanor was already better known to the Greeks and her influence more often sought than that of my superiors. She had a taste for languages too and never confused the Embassy staff with English either in Athens or later in Alexandria. People naturally saw things her way because she went more than halfway to meet them. Being beautiful did no harm either.' He was smiling now, and slowly sipping his drink.

'Where did you meet?'

'London, just after World War I. She was working as an intern in Guy's and her mother sent me to see her because I'd been home on leave from the Army. The old girl was worried about the company Eleanor was keeping in London. They thought she was going to marry some medical chap from Ceylon and I was asked to go and advise her against it on religious grounds. I hardly knew her except to see – no young fellow in this town could fail to know Eleanor by sight in those days. She was Clara Bow and Maud Gonne and the Queen of Sheba all rolled into one. She'd take the eyes out of your head if she so much as scratched her eyebrow during Mass. She was bad for the soul, I can tell you that.'

'I bet she laughed when you trotted out her mother's advice.'

'Of course she did, the way any girl with a bit of spirit in her would. But we became great friends, because in one way I think she was lonely. She hated this town as she does to this day, but she missed it all the same, and all the life of the old house. We became engaged next summer when we were both going home on holidays.'

'But the boy from Ceylon?'

'As Eleanor said, the rumours about him that reached home were greatly exaggerated. It fizzled out, whatever was between them, and she married me the year I was appointed to Athens. That was the summer of twenty-four. '

The silence that fell between us as we both sipped the drinks was entirely companionable and I hardly liked to break it. But I might never get an opportunity again. 'Were you happy?'

The question could be taken as he pleased, happy in Greece, happy to be appointed, happy with Eleanor. I could also be asking was she happy too. With one of the quick covert looks by which you can pick out a Corkman anywhere, Con let me know that he knew what I was really asking him. And he laughed.

'I was a simple fellow in those days. I was happy and I thought she was. She was in full bloom and I had an allowance that could rise to all the gauzy dresses and all the fa-lals that sort of life required. No other woman in the room had a chance anywhere when Eleanor walked in.'

I had heard, of course, versions of this life from Eleanor. The time he had burnt a cigarette hole in her bridal nightgown which was pure silk with five hundred little pin-tucks. The time he had arrived unwashed from the mountains to meet the Duke of Gloucester who was touring in the Royal yacht. The time he had lost a thousand pounds in two nights at poker. Now Con's pause was so long I was sorry I'd spoken, but tried to make up for it by talking on.

'She's often told me about how she loved Greece, loved the people especially. She compared them to Irish country people once you get away from the cities, generous in a princely way with whatever they have, however little. She told me how hard it was to pay for anything, from a meal or night's lodging to a donkey ride in the heat of the day even when the owner would have to walk himself. She told me the only thing to do was never go into the country without a supply of some luxury – cigarettes, good chocolate, but especially Scotch whisky.'

'And don't forget, her professional skill,' Con said, 'I don't suppose she told you she'd never take payment either – although mind you, she loves money.' I didn't tell him I knew that. 'She delivered more babies in goatherds' stone hovels all over the place than you would believe possible. Weekends if things were quiet we usually went into the mountains. There was always somebody who would lend us a house. Eleanor loved walking, and I, as you know, can take it or leave it. In the heat of those incredible summers of the 'twenties there were things I preferred doing to scrambling like a goat over rocks that cut you like glass under a sun that would dry up the very brains inside your head.

Eleanor needed only the slightest excuse to be off, alone or with anybody we might have staying with us. And she usually carried a hip flask of Irish whisky as a dual-purpose disinfectant in a countryside where hygiene was unheard of in those days. Still is, to some extent, in remote places. She once stitched a badly torn young woman who had been taken unawares and delivered herself of twins on the side of a mountain near Mycenae, golden Mycenae. Eleanor had nothing but whisky to fight the infection.'

I knew this story. Eleanor was proud of it. 'Do you know what that shepherd's wife called one of the boys?' I knew this too, but the delighted look of him even so long afterward made me shake my head.

'She called him Cornelius Menelaus,' Con chuckled, 'after me. I went over to see her next day with Eleanor. The other twin was Agamemnon. Imagine it, Ruth. Somewhere out there on the Greek mainland under that burning sky there's a Con and an Agamemnon walking around to this day, and Con is the exotic one. Breeding up a long sturdy line of Cons and Agamemnons I have no doubt.'

Con's laughter stopped abruptly when he noticed the time. It was half an hour beyond our usual lunchtime and he was as nervous as any schoolboy hurrying home late, knowing punishment would follow. I hate family quarrels, particularly other people's. Peaceable enough myself, it has often seemed to me that trouble follows me around like a stray dog. It did that day. Even so many years afterwards, I shiver when I consider the ferocity of the scene on our return.

The family was sitting anxiously around the table giving us five minutes more before beginning the main part of the meal. My mother-in-law Margaret brushed aside our late arrival and so even did Hanny after our breathless apologies, but Eleanor, who had done the cooking that day, was furious. She ignored me completely and attacked Con with such savagery that I thought he couldn't possibly pass it over and sit down with us. He did, however. He sat between the shocked speechless Julia and myself and we tried to get on with the meal as though nothing had happened.

The earthenware pot Eleanor had brought to the table contained a superb slow-cooked beef stew which couldn't possibly have come to any harm even if we had been a couple of hours instead of forty-five minutes late, but nobody really had any relish for it except Eleanor herself and, to my astonishment, Con.

Smiling broadly, he told story after story about his Egyptian days while clearing the plate with the greatest relish. Neither he nor Eleanor had ever lost the capacity to eat elegantly and talk at the same time, but Eleanor would not utter a word that day. White hair curling glossily above the handsome dark eyes, she sat up stiffly in the single shaft of light coming through the jungly window. She sat self-contained and scornful as a cat throughout the meal but roused herself to bustling action when we had finished. My attempt to help clear away was icily rejected and in no time at all she had the kitchen cleared except for Julia who would no doubt suffer while Eleanor read the Irish Times, only lifting her head to direct operations.

It was late afternoon before she would speak to me again, and then it was as if nothing whatever had happened. I was getting ready to walk the five or six miles around the estuary to meet Martin on his way down for the weekend. This was Friday, and it was no penance to liberate myself into the evening light and watch for the car on the high road from which you could look across the harbour at the town. The boys' grandmother had already offered to put them to bed, so Eleanor was late with that offer.

'But thanks very much all the same, Eleanor.'

'You know perfectly well it's a pleasure,' she said impatiently, 'They're probably the nearest thing to grandchildren I'll ever have. I'll read to them if they'd like that?'

'They'd love it. We're halfway through Samuel Whiskers. You can finish it if you like.'

'Dear Beatrix Potter,' Eleanor smiled, 'Julia had all those lovely books read and re-read to her by her nurse in Athens. She should have turned out better.'

'Why don't you give Julia a chance, Eleanor? She's kind-hearted and dependable and full of goodwill towards everybody.'

'She's stupid,' Eleanor snapped, 'stupid and clumsy and dull as ditchwater. And she has no guts. If she had she wouldn't be here at all. She'd have a career like everybody else.'

'But if she were somebody else's daughter instead of yours you'd kindly try to work out what her problems may have been – and are. Wouldn't you?'

'Her problem is that she's Con's daughter with serfdom in her blood. His sisters who grew up in that hovel I showed you were no better than cows. In due course they served their biological function – no more. Julia was built for a purpose she will probably never serve!'

Then I knew I didn't really belong here. I hate family quarrels, as I said. I began to realise the extent of the damage people could do to one another without ever realising it. I felt isolated and vaguely threatened, and then I remembered I was actually on my way to meet Martin, who was born of these people and knew them to the bone. So long as he was here the cruel games they played with one another could never touch me. To my astonishment, as though she could read my mind, Eleanor laughed, kissed me affectionately and left me as far as the door, an arm flung around my shoulder.

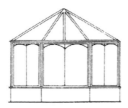

There are things about that woman I will never understand, about Hanny, I mean. The creaking door. The small sickly baby who was not going to make it into her twenties and who therefore had to be cosseted by her mama Julia and by old Maurice. Sometimes I think that dislike of Hanny is the only bond left between Eleanor and me. The unmitigated contrariness of the woman. Take the little matter of the kitchen door this morning. The lock has been hard to turn for days and Hanny's hands in particular are as fragile as a bird's claws. It's been in my mind since before Martin and Ruth arrived to get a new tin of lubricating oil and set it to rights. In this house it has always been the custom to replace empty tins and bottles on the shelf so that nobody can ever know when some commodity or other needs to be replaced. Anyhow yesterday I found the tin was empty and bought a new one in the town. Quite pleased with myself for remembering it as a matter of fact. Big deal. And this morning bright and early I had just set about oiling the lock when Hanny came down the stairs to the kitchen. Eyed me with displeasure.

'Playing about again, Con, for want of something better to do,' she greets me kindly. 'Have a care would you damage that lock, good strong old article though it is.'

'I'm being kind to it, Hanny. Giving it a drink of oil after it's been dying of drought for months.'

'That's not the right sort of oil, though – you'll ruin it. You got that tin in O'Connor's. 'Tis Fitzgerald's have the right stuff.'

'That last tin of oil was probably bought in O'Connor's some time around 1934. This is the only sort of stuff you can get anywhere after all these years. And it's first class.'

'O'Connor is not a man I like to do business with all the same – we never gave him our custom in this house since he voted in De Valera and caused the Economic War.'

'Look, Hanny, the job's done now. Open the door for yourself and see how easy it is.'

'It's too easy, so it is. In a gale of wind that lock might open all by itself and somebody would have to get up to shut it. And if you were wearing a white dress a drop of that dark old oil would destroy you.'

As though on cue, Ruth came down the stairs wearing not a white dress but white cotton trousers that went well with the long legs. It seems no time since she came here that summer with the month-old twins who are big lads at school now.

'Have a care, Ruth, would you ruin your clothes with the dirty old oil Con has plastered all over the kitchen lock. I'll get the kettle on.'

Hanny vanished disgruntled into the kitchen, the door closing sweetly behind her. Ruth and I exchanged smiles and good mornings. She looked slightly worried.

'I dropped in on Eleanor when I was on my way down. I think she wants something but I couldn't make out what. Will you go to her, Con?'

'I'll go up right away. But I thought she was all right when I left her.'

'Poor Eleanor,' the girl said. She bit her lip and I saw the tears in her eyes. She and Martin had heard about Eleanor but not seen her until this summer. Ruth was about to say something else when her sons came trampling downstairs calling to her about having a swim before breakfast.

She smiled apologetically at me after agreeing to go with them and I went up to Eleanor. Julia was there already in the big sun-filled room, brown eyes fixed in concern on her mother, who of course gestured to me to get her out of the way.

'I'll see to your mother, Julia.' Only too used to dismissal, Julia went. I looked in the strong light thrown up from the harbour at the ruins of Eleanor.

She sat straight against a wall of pillows in the small wrought-iron bed that had been hers as a child. Since the stroke that robbed her of speech and of all movement along the right side of her body including her face, she had lost about two stone in weight. The hand that could move beat in impatience on the white bedspread. In the twisted face only the eye muscles could work properly. If you covered that face from the nose down it might even be mistaken for Eleanor's again – it was always the eyes you noticed first anyhow, huge, black, brilliant and impatient. They were so now because she was uttering sounds I could make no sense of. I fetched and held a notepad for her, then put a pencil between the fingers of the one good hand. On an impulse I bent and kissed her forehead. The eyes furiously denied my right to do that, and she wrote on the pad, 'Send Martin to me'.

'You know Martin, Eleanor. Sleeps like the dead for the first few mornings of his holiday. Not even the twins can waken him and Ruth leaves him be. I'll try to rouse him if you like.'

She wrote: 'Later'. When she closed her eyes as she did now she looked corpse-like but the doctor had said she might recover, regain at least some movement on the right side. She waved me away with her eyes still closed, then changed her mind and gestured at her tray by the bedside. I knew Hanny had fed her earlier from that tray – she would never allow me to do it – and of course I ought to have remembered myself to take it down. On the other hand, not having done so gave Eleanor the pleasure of despising me again and she had so few pleasures left. I touched the good hand in farewell before taking the tray away and as usual felt the refusal of my touch in her very bones. No thunderbolt from the gods such as this could ever entirely change Eleanor.

Increasingly now (and it's probably the sign of old age in me) I think of her in London as she was when old Julia sent me to save her from a mixed marriage. I didn't relish raising a private matter with the proud beauty who would hardly nod to me in the main street at home. I asked the old lady why she thought Eleanor would pay the slightest attention to me, if she would listen at all. Her mother laughed.

'Aren't you like a son coming into this house, Con, whenever you're at home? – why wouldn't she listen?'

'At least, ma'am, give me some reason for calling on her in London.'

'You could take her this,' old Julia said, swooping on a piece of linen on top of her workbox between the two big windows of the drawing-room. She often worked there, never missing anybody passing in the street below. Her lacework was locally famous, done for the nuns when the family were young, to add to old Maurice's savings. They were both ambitious for a finer house. It was said she often sat up until three in the morning to finish some piece or other for which the nuns would pay her a pittance but the pittances added up. She would be up again at half past six to get the children ready for school. I looked at the cobweb of fine linen and lace she was parcelling up for me.

'I wonder . . .?' I began doubtfully.

'Eleanor will be glad of that whenever she makes a cup of tea for a friend in her room at the hospital. It's a little tray cloth I made last week and she'll appreciate it, because she was never a one to use her own hands,' old Julia chuckled briskly. 'I'm grateful to you, Con,' she said then, smiling in a way that even in her old age recalled her daughter to me.

'What I was going to say . . .' I began again and stopped. It seemed possible to me that Eleanor might regard the little gift as a go-ahead, something for her bottom drawer, in the manner of those days. On the other hand it was at least an excuse for calling on her. I shook hands with Eleanor's mother and was about to go when she seized me by both elbows and looked down kindly into my face – a tall handsome woman in her mid-sixties, whose last child Eleanor had come as an afterthought, as she often said herself.

'Your mother told us about your promotion over in London and we're as pleased about it as she is herself, Con. If ever you did in truth become a member of the family, wouldn't we have the big welcome for you!'

So that was it. Better the divil you know even if he does come of humble origins than a black stranger (literally) from big dangerous London via Ceylon. Hanny appeared suddenly to show me downstairs – even as a young girl she was birdlike and usually dressed in grey. She had a habit of scanning you sideways from the hazel eyes and finding you lacking. Today she looked spruce in one of her mother's lace collars over the grey dress.

'What did they promote you to?' she asked me tartly on the way downstairs. 'Office boy?'

'I've in fact gone a few steps higher in the Foreign Office if you'd believe it, Hanny.'

'Sure if you tell me so I have to believe it. Aren't you a credit to us all in the town! What do they call you now over beyond in London?'

'Too early in the morning.' I chanced the old joke and she raked me with the little eyes.

'No, but really?'

'First Secretary,' I said.

'Oh, then you type the letters so for them to send out foreign. I see,' Hanny said, lips pursed up and eyes very wicked in the small face.

45

'Goodbye, Hanny.'

'Tell Eleanor to come home without fail for the Regatta,' she said, letting me out into the windy sunlight which I was glad to breathe in quickly. 'Tell her not to miss it like last year.'

When I told Eleanor a few weeks later she looked as nearly wistful as that sort of face could ever look. 'The Regatta,' she said, 'I'd nearly forgotten.'

She moved smiling around her room in Guy's Hospital, a cluttered room with a big mahogany desk on which she had already arranged the daffodils I brought her. Eleanor at that stage tended to make young men speechless but old men gallant and garrulous. Her face was beautiful and difficult to remember exactly five minutes after you left her. What you did remember were the extraordinary eyes and the way you felt when they caught and held yours. Different. Almighty. Changed for better or worse but (you fancied) for ever.

'How are they, Con?' She held up her mother's present to the murky light from a tall window, and she smiled. 'I have dozens of these. She forgets every time she sends me one. How are they, Con?'

'Well, I think. Looking forward to Margaret and everybody coming home in the summer. A bit anxious about you, I think.'

'Oh. Why?'

This was it, and how to phrase it? Because a young

46

one from the town saw you with a black man on the river in Richmond? Because Aggie Donovan has a friend who works in your own hospital kitchens who wrote back to say that Eleanor O'Donohue was great with an Indian doctor qualified the same year as herself and would probably marry and go foreign with him? Because?

'I think because they believe London is big and lonely and you might fall in with the wrong company.'

'Oh God!' Eleanor said, elbows on her desk, head bent over into her hands, laughing helplessly. 'So they know. Of course they'd know – the bush telegraph! What is the wrong company, Con? Tell me?'

'Anybody they don't know around the streets of Ferrycarrig since he was a boy, I suppose. Please don't blame me, Eleanor. I called to see them when I was home on leave and your mother asked me to – to come and give you her love.'

'You lie very badly, Con. It's appealing, for some reason.'

'Then,' – quickly, before hope dies! – 'why don't you come and have dinner with me one evening next week? Please.'

'Do you know I'm tempted to say yes. This is a first class hospital but the food is vile.'

It was that evening which finally fixed her face in my mind for ever. I could call it up in detail anywhere, any time, and I sometimes do it still. Over a drink in

McNallys. Up on the roof looking for loose slates after a storm. I look over the churned waters of the harbour and I see the face of a twenty-four-year-old girl which changed completely very soon after I married her for a reason I have never known. Nobody else ever noticed. Beautiful Eleanor, they said, always the same, whatever happens to the rest of us.

I don't complain, I never did. It is not easy to accept what has happened to her now but I don't feel useless because the old house itself needs my hand to keep it going. I seldom see it in winter but I spend two or three months of every summer here, as Eleanor and I have always done. Our house in Cork is closed up every year in June, and down we come to pick up the threads of a life which seems to have changed very little in two generations. The three sisters, Eleanor and Margaret and Hanny, come together again, become locked into a relationship that hasn't changed since they were children. Margaret, Martin's mother, used to come down from Cork with her husband and children every year. Now that he is dead and the children scattered she lives here, welcomes Martin and Ruth and their children every summer, sees another cycle beginning, and is happy. The calmest and kindest of the three sisters, she showed steel only once in her life. That was six years after our young Julia was born and Eleanor wanted to adopt Martin and take him back to Alexandria where we were posted then. Margaret had married a weakling and never had enough money to keep going. Eleanor said that Martin (whom she had delivered in this very house) must have the best that could be provided for him, and his mother had to pinch and scrape to survive in Cork. The boy should be given a chance, Eleanor kept saying. Margaret stood firm and Eleanor never forgave her.

On the other hand Margaret and Hanny, when alone, often slip into the sort of chatter of two older sisters about a spoiled and pretty young one, exclaiming over her latest escapade, shaking their heads, but more in envy than in disapproval. What will she do next, etc. Now that Eleanor is blighted, chained in rage to her little iron bed, they both wait devotedly on her and on their demented mother who still lives in a world where scheming women are forever trying to get at her tall clever sons, all of whom are dead. Like so many who grew up in this British naval base two of them were lost at sea during the First World War. Two others, who were academics, drank themselves into an early grave: so that old Julia, who lives on for ever, has two obsessions. The other one is alcohol. Drink is forbidden in the house. When you go out for a jar, you have gone for a walk, and you mustn't forget it. Young Ruth thought it hilarious when first she came here with Martin, but she's used to it now. Julia dodders on – she must be well over the century by now – never knowing which generation is coming down for the summer, glad so long as the house keeps comparatively full. Her room beside the first-floor drawing-room is jammed with fine needlework. Some time I must suggest to her to cover her walls with petit-point instead of paper. That should keep her going for the rest of her life, as the maintenance of her house will keep me going.

Maybe because I'm only here on occasional Sundays in winter, I take greater care to anticipate trouble during the summer. The hotter the day the more likely I am to go up on the roof and walk carefully along the valley, looking for weak points. I tighten slates when they are only thinking of coming loose. I clean and paint gutters. I watch for subsidence and I always find it. Two years ago I rebuilt a chimney stack and marvelled at the hard work of men dead for two hundred years. It's a good house. Old Maurice bought it as evidence of a successful life in public service but he died a few years afterwards. He had the satisfaction however of being waked in great splendour, laid out in his wife's best handiwork linen. I, who grew up in a two-roomed cabin at the paupers' end of town, maintain the fine house he bought in good time to die in. His daughter, the creaking door, does not thank me for it but then why should she? We are all passengers in her eyes except herself and her mother Julia, but she knows she couldn't do without us. She and Margaret and old Julia gather up their feathers and somehow sit out the winter. If they can survive there will be warmth and company and gossip and sun coming through open windows again, so they survive. Margaret gets more frail to look at, Julia gets always crazier, but Hanny remains triumphantly the same, the fragile premature baby who refused to die, the same elderly young girl mocking at the world in general, the despiser of men who was at least consistent and never married, the owner after old Julia of this fine old house: the creaking door, as the locals say. One of my nightmares is that they will all die or otherwise go away and only Hanny and I will be left who can live neither with nor without one another. Even her army of cats out in the yard sits and glares in stony dislike at me through the scullery window. By the way, I made a new draining board of sheet metal in that scullery because the wood of the old one was rotten, but Hanny never used it. Sniffed at it and said she supposed everything would slide off it, and dried the ware item by item rather than use it. Margaret admired it and said we'd destroy the nice shine of it if we put damp ware on it. She never used it herself either, and young Julia broke a cup the first day she dried up from it, and that was that.

Never in my life in any house have I heard the sort of uproar that follows the breaking of a cup in this house. There are more cups and saucers and ware of

51

every kind, 'good' and everyday, than all of us will ever be able to use even if each of us were to break a piece a day, but it doesn't make any difference. The uproar is always the same and it is usually young Julia who brings it crashing about her innocent head.

Julia? Her trouble is that she must have been born feeling in the wrong. Only boys' names were ready and waiting for her. It never for a moment crossed Eleanor's head that she might not be carrying a son, and when the fact was proved by Julia's birth one burning noonday in Athens, she shook her head in disbelief and asked the nurses to take the ugly little thing away. She hardly looked at her again until young Julia was four or five. She was reared by a succession of Greek nurses – a 'good' child who was awkward and clumsy as she grew up but never deliberately troublesome.

I went up to play with her every evening and was satisfied that in Athens of all places she could not have been better looked after. The Greeks young and old, male and female, love children and will spend endless time with them.

Outside this old house is the town, and with it I have come to terms long ago. It is an old and beautiful and suspicious town, once a rich port that traded with France and Spain and had its quota of merchant gentry loyal to the English crown. Its sons very often joined the British Navy, trained in Portsmouth, like two of Eleanor's brothers, came home with braided uniforms and smart manners, pitied those who remained and were much in demand for regatta parties. They perished in their hundreds during two wars but their hopeful young faces under braided caps look at you from photographs on mantelpiece or piano all over town. Heroes of the Irish War of Independence are more likely to have come from the hills and villages to the west. Their peasant faces are reproduced in stone on town memorials in the market square. Framed copies of their last letters to relatives from the death cell are not uncommon in the part of town where I was born, but on the whole Ferrycarrig remained British and conservative. I have my place now among the town elders in the bar of the Royal Hotel because despite low origins I served at the highest diplomatic level under the right Government and could afford to come home with a new suit and good suitcases every year, accompanied by a wife who was the daughter of their County Manager. I never remember anybody in town ever calling Eleanor by my name. She was 'Dr O'Donohue as I always think of you' to virtually the whole town. She didn't quarrel with that. She has been married to me for all these years and lived all over the world, but that house in Ferrycarrig is still incontrovertibly her home. Now that she is stricken, I doubt if she will ever leave it again.

And meanwhile? The little universe that is the

town fascinates me quite as much as the world outside. I only see it spruced up for summer, freshly painted after the annual procession, beflagged for the Regatta, full of flowering plants in little tubs and old gas lights (recently reprieved) gilded and burnished. I only see brown faces and summer dresses, and ever since I was sixteen or seventeen this is more or less all I have ever seen. Winter is a different place. I try to imagine this town closed and shuttered for winter, people muffled up into high collars against the cold, and I cannot. Yet I know the anatomy of the houses and I know that each has a stout oak board for fitting in grooves outside the door when the winter tides rise. Sandbags are laid against the board inside, and that way the hall stays fairly dry. But I believe I am right in thinking that the winter life of this town is merely time-marking, not to be taken too seriously. You survive, and then it will be summer again. Ferrycarrig has been a self-conscious little resort for most of two hundred years.

I do remember being here one early spring by myself while Eleanor was taking a briefing course at some hospital or other and one of her brothers was home on leave from the Navy. That was Alex, who had carefully dried himself out before coming home. He wanted to leave a little of his labour behind for us to remember him by so he decided to build a summerhouse and put it up in the garden for his mother. It was some time in the thirties, in the very infancy of the wretched Do It Yourself craze (few people are born with the patience I have for such hard work). Alex had seen an advertisement saying 'Build your own summerhouse' in some magazine or other, and he set up his workshop in a little room off the kitchen where the cook-general used to sleep when they had a cook-general. The weather was raw and sleety in early March, and this summerhouse was a pretty thing of fretwork with a little pointed roof, made for clematis and rambler roses. You were advised to make it indoors and then get help to carry it out to its permanent position in the garden where you would have prepared the foundations. I offered to do this bit while Alex laboured indoors, ordering people to head his mother off if she enquired what all the hammering was about. Even then, she spent most of her days upstairs and rarely went out, so it wasn't too difficult. Alex laboured on, sneered at by Hanny who said the summerhouse would collapse when we tried to carry it out, and encouraged by me since it was difficult for him to drink and work with hammer and chisel at the same time.

'Do you think the base maybe is a bit broad for that doorway, Alex?' I said to him one day, making a quick eye-measurement.

'Not at all, old man,' said Alex, 'I did careful calculations before I began. All we have to do is get it through slightly on the diagonal. Of course we'll have to get help from the Horgan boys with the whole removal operation.'

Happily he worked on as March became April (cold and wild still) and April brought Easter and after that soft winds and apple blossom up in the garden. You approach that garden by mounting four steps from the stone-flagged yard which is full of cats and plant pots. The day we decided to move the summerhouse, Hanny caught and put the cats in a large laundry basket from which fearful howls emerged, and then, helped by Julia, she moved the plant pots into the outside lavatory so that we couldn't damage any of them. Among the earthen pots were old kettles and saucepans full of budding life, anything into which the green fingers of Hanny could put down a slip.

At last all was ready. The two Horgan boys shook their heads at the sight of the summerhouse in the inner room, obviously agreeing with me that it was hardly possible to remove it through the door, and Alex began to flutter in his fashion as the big moment arrived. He called on us to admire the fretwork around the gothic-style windows, the smooth gliding motion of the little pointed door. The Horgan boys suggested what I would have done myself, that we try to get it head first on its side through the door. Outside in the stone-flagged kitchen, in the filtered green light from the yard,

Martin's mother Margaret stood with an anxious hand over her mouth and Hanny was beside her, hands on hips, lips pursed, little eyes sparkling with the happy certainty of disaster. Young Julia looked through the kitchen window from the yard, like a girl watching a play. I wished I wasn't so certain the thing couldn't be done, but I might be wrong all the same. I hoped I was wrong.

All went well until we came to the base. There was no possible way that it could go through the door until Alex, fevered by now, began to mark two triangular pieces on the door frame. He ordered us to move his Taj Mahal back again, and then before anybody could stop him he began to hack the two triangular bits out of the door frame with a small handsaw. Hanny shrieked like a startled hen, but Alex said he would replace the little segments so neatly with the right sort of adhesive that nobody would ever be able to notice that they had been removed in the first place. There's no doubt that he was right about how to get the summerhouse through. Within minutes it was lying on its side on the kitchen floor and the Horgans were spitting on their sore hands and looking with even more dubiousness at the side door into the yard through which the thing also had to go. But wait, we were wrong. Alex said the next thing was to pull up the lower sash of the kitchen window as far as it would go and get the summerhouse out that way. Two men would have to go outside and two stay in. A bit of pulling and pushing would do the trick.

By the time this plan had been reduced to the patent impossibility it was, Alex was close to tears and the women had fled from the kitchen. One of the Horgans suggested we adjourn (leaving the summerhouse resting like a collapsed pavilion on the floor) to the local hostelry for a pint each since we would require all our strength for the next move. I believed the next move should be the dismantling of the structure to its component parts to be put together again by all of us up in the garden, but Alex wouldn't hear of it: the thing wasn't put together with nails or screws but pegged and glued with some new wonder adhesive so it was really just one huge indivisible piece. We missed him after the first pint in the corner pub, and again my prophetic soul told me where he might be. I was right. Alex was back in the yard, working in a frenzy with axe and sledgehammer on the window frame. A heap of rubble was all around him inside and outside, and Margaret was crying. Hanny, when we arrived, was beating him with her little fists about the hips (the only part of his body she could easily get at) and there was nothing to do but take charge.

'Stop acting like a fool this minute, Alex, and give over before you bring the entire back wall down!' I shouted, and motioned the Horgans to go and take the weapons from him. The Horgans were heavier and as big as he was and there were two of them.

Disarmed, Alex went away blubbering and we spent the rest of that day with sawn beams, nails, chisels and plaster to repair the wreckage. The window sash was functioning again by evening and we stood up the summerhouse in a corner of the huge kitchen until Alex could decide what to do about it. It is there to this day, startling strangers who see it for the first time, used for hanging clothes to dry in during the winter, and quite pretty if crazy-looking with Hanny's plants hung from hooks and trailing around its sides.

Alex went on a binge from which it took him a fortnight to recover, and I spent one evening before he went away drinking pot after pot of coffee with him in the Royal Hotel. I tried to avoid the subject of the summerhouse but Alex wanted to talk about it, and indeed about other sore subjects. His red eyes peered at me from the puffy folds of flesh, and he looked suddenly old.

'That house is a sort of graveyard,' he said at last. 'They bury things there that they find inconvenient. Take Janet for instance.' In her day I would have taken Janet at any time, as fair and friendly a lady as you would find in a day's walk, but the wrong nationality, the wrong religion, the wrong sort of young woman for this house since she had had the brazenness to marry their Alex without asking their leave.

'The first time I sailed the Pacific she stayed here with the baby until I could join them for the end of the summer. Full of spunk and optimism – you remember her, Con? And they beat her down, they nagged the life out of her that summer. Froze her out. Offered to take and keep the baby Andrew and let her go back to her people. Wanted to have him baptised a Catholic and even brought the priest to see her in the drawing-room. She was gone when I came home, and nothing was ever the same again.'

'Long-distance marriages are always difficult anyway, Alex. Might have happened whether she came here or not.'

'It would not,' Alex said fiercely, and rang the bell for a double brandy. After a few sips he looked himself again. 'I haven't set foot in this house since then, but this year Margaret wrote to tell me how frail Mama was getting so I thought I'd come for the few free months and leave something behind me that she would enjoy and maybe think better of me for giving her. It's a graveyard, that house. You walk in tall on your feet and you end up flattened again. You end up a joke. Would you do something for me, Con?'

'If I can.'

'Smash up the summerhouse and light the fires with it. That's the best way to forget about the whole thing.'

'They mightn't let me, Alex. Remember I'm an outsider like Janet.' He shrugged, already appearing to forget what he'd asked me when he was into his second double brandy.

I mention the whole ludicrous incident because of what it was that Alex wanted to give his mother to remember him by. A summerhouse. The house in Ferrycarrig itself was that, a place you thought about in a sentimental haze when you were away but which sucked you back disastrously into its meshes when you were here. Alex was accidentally torpedoed by one of his own ships in the Bay of Biscay and lost his life. Janet was killed soon afterwards in an air raid on London and their son Andrew was at last caught into the trap of Ferrycarrig when Eleanor and I adopted him. There are aspects of his life in this house that I'd rather not dwell on.

What sort of picture have I painted anyhow that leaves out Ruth and Martin, the pair who get away unharmed and unchanged every year, who come again and again to the summerhouse? They belong I think to the entire generation who got away – away from religion, conventional morality, sacred cows of every kind. They didn't for instance have a wedding, not so anybody would notice. She put on a summer dress and he a tie and they signed their names at the Registry Office in Dublin. At that time I knew, although the rest of this house probably did not, they had been living together for almost two years. After the ceremony at the Registry Office, they cooked spaghetti at the flat for the two witnesses and themselves, packed their rucksacks, and went off to Greece. The only reason this house forgave them is that she obviously wasn't pregnant: the boys were born two years afterwards. They are still as easy in one another's company as two people recently introduced who have taken a liking to one another. They may even be in love still. A couple of years ago I remember a blazing afternoon in August when Martin was joining her after Ruth had been here with the babies for a week or so. I saw her drying her hair in the sun that morning and later ironing a blue cotton dress in the kitchen. She was singing like a lark. You felt if you touched her, happiness would come away like pollen on your fingers.

I watched her later with a canvas bag slung over her shoulder, swinging off to walk the six miles by the estuary to the crossroads where two counties meet. She proposed to sit in the sun by the river with a book and wait for Martin to come by unawares. She waited, she told me afterwards, for two hours and then she recognised at once the sound of his ancient Peugeot engine and she went over to thumb a lift. He thought she was a hitchhiker and stopped to take her up. He was partly blinded by the setting sun, driving west, and that was how they met again. They come and they go but the house at Ferrycarrig never touches them. They are kind, especially Ruth. They even cry like children sometimes over our miseries – I've seen tears in both their eyes speaking of Eleanor – but they will not be enmeshed. They are free souls.

I think the nearest Ruth ever came to trying to change anything in this house was the evening she asked me to go for a walk with her – out past the old Abbey and the town walls which I climbed as a child. She wanted to talk about Andrew. She didn't know that she had already changed something for me, irrevocably. I shall try to piece together the early morning scene which made Ruth determined to talk to me. She had fed the babies at five o'clock and instead of going back to bed she decided on a swim because the sun was welling up over the harbour and the tide was on the turn. It was six o'clock of a July morning and the town was still asleep.

'I love mornings,' Ruth said. As she talked I saw her in my mind's eye, twenty-five years old, floating free on a full tide, eyes closed but smiling. As she said, crowded beaches were several hours away. The two babies were fed and safely asleep. She was free and she loves mornings. I saw her treading water as the sun strengthened, wet hair shaken back, eyes streaming but fixed on the tiered pretty town, old walls black and broken against the morning sky, the cathedral spire sharp and silvery above them and in layers down to the waterfront the roofs and chimney stacks of blue slate. My town, not hers. Around the cobblestoned docks old houses leaned together in a jumble of architectural styles, but all painted sprucely now (after the annual procession) in marine blues, or a variety of reds and yellows. She swam in, and at the boatslip she could see the open window with its looped lace curtains behind which her sons slept. That house is one of the tall spindly ones built together towards the close of the eighteenth century, handsome pikehead railings protecting their lower windows from the cattle on fair days and from passers-by at all times. The house old Maurice bought to prove how far above the rest of us he was.

But I'm rambling. I don't suppose old Maurice would ever have passed through Ruth's mind. I'm just trying to stand where she stood, treading water that untouched summer's morning, and see my town through her eyes. If she looked to the right from this house she saw, in the direction of the dock, fishermen's houses whitewashed and gleaming, half-doors shortly to be opened to let loose the tumbling hordes of small children. As she gazed back at the town, some women would surely have got the fires going. Turfsmoke would curl from the squat little chimneys and eddy out into the harbour pungent and homely. Ruth would have hung suspended in the water for a while, still tasting the morning, unwilling to let the day begin because she loved this feeling of being free and entirely alone. Suddenly a boy emerged from nowhere and dived off the harbour wall, a clumsy bellyflopper of a dive that sounded in the glassy stillness like a gunshot. He swam better than he dived and suddenly he surfaced quite near her after a longish swim underwater. Under flaming hair his familiar adolescent pimples were cruelly hot and bright (she said) in the sunshine, some of them with infected heads. But his streaming face was full of smiles. Eyes cast down (I think because she hated to criticise) Ruth told me she noticed that even his white teeth were crooked and prominent; a little dental care could have made them presentable, still could if anybody cared enough.

She said hello to him and Andrew said, 'Hello, Ruthie, I watched you from the window above and I said to myself if she goes swimming I will too, matteradamn what they say.' I smiled because she got the vulgar local accent he affected at that time. She asked him why shouldn't he go swimming before breakfast if he felt like it, and again, as she reported his words, I heard the loutish resentful tones coming through.

'She says I have to study before breakfast so she does, to try and keep up with the other fellows next term – she bought me an alarm clock last week and set it for six o'clock. I can go swimming after I've done out their room, run messages for Aunt Margaret and polished all the shoes for them . . .'

'Why, Con,' Ruth said, 'do you allow it? He's your son now, freely adopted, yours and Eleanor's. Why, Con?'

Why? Why? Because it's easier to let her have her own way. It always has been. What Ruth should have asked and indeed did ask later was why Eleanor chose to regard both Andrew and her own Julia as inferior beings rather than members of the family. Why? Ruth was waiting for an answer and I couldn't find the right words except in my own mind. Eleanor's daughter (if she had to have one) should have been beautiful and original, worthy of her. People should have looked at them strolling together in the sunshine and smiled, making jokes about the two sisters. As it was (and even abroad) people tended not to believe that the pale silent Julia with her apprehensive bun face could possibly be a daughter of Eleanor's. And Andrew? His father was a fool and a drunk, his mother an outsider – what could you expect? He had for his own good to be curbed and disciplined if she was ever to make a man of him. His teeth? I honestly don't think Eleanor ever noticed them – she looked at him as little as possible. And if I had had those teeth seen to I would be expected to foot the bill out of my own pocket – Eleanor had grown increasingly tight-fisted with money. It was as simple as that. Laissez faire.

It wasn't as brutal as Ruth seemed to think. I genuinely felt that Andrew in a few years time would have clear skin and good teeth like anybody else's. I also knew that as usual I was taking the line of least resistance. I was sorry that Ruth whom I loved was so upset about the boy. But I didn't really see what I could do about it. There was another thing of course. Andrew represented for Eleanor her own failure to produce anything better. He was our son because we didn't have a son. And so, never deliberately but gradually bit by bit he was neglected, and my occasional bursts of guilt and generosity did him no good whatever. Andrew was my failure just as much as Eleanor's. I didn't thank him for it.

But what was stranger than his emotional rejection by us (and let's be clear, that's what it was) what was infinitely stranger was the attitude of Margaret (normally as kind a soul as you could hope to meet) and Hanny to him. Eleanor, as I said, hardly saw him any more. Margaret and Hanny actively disliked him. Margaret's children, of whom Ruth's Martin was the plum, were civil, clever, and charming. Always cherished, they had never been punished because, as Margaret often pointed out, they never needed it. They passed their exams punctually and brilliantly and they did everybody credit. Their certificates, diplomas, degrees were filed away proudly in the cabinet upstairs – typically, in this house, not in their own house. Andrew, on the other hand, had difficulty right from the beginning. When he first came down with Eleanor and me, the summer we adopted him, he had a grating English accent and was laughed at by local children. He was sneered at by Hanny when in self-defence he adopted the local accent. Nobody in this house had ever quite spoken in the accents of the town. The rhythms were the same and many of the expressions were similar, but they spoke grammatically and they did not drawl. Andrew picked up every nuance of the dock area, and indeed such friends as he had lived down there. He was forbidden to bring them to the house, and in the places where they lived, children from outside the family were not encouraged into the houses which were too small to house themselves anyway. 'Craic' took place at street corners. Andrew quickly picked up not only the accent but the very wriggle of the arse affected by the local young fellows. After some initial efforts to make him change his friends, his Aunt Margaret joined Hanny in regarding him as an unsalvageable lout, some sort of a throwback to the family's peasant origins.

However, to give Margaret her due, she helped him with his schoolwork in the beginning and she certainly taught him enough Irish to make him do no worse at it than at any other subject. He was not what could be called bright, and as less and less was expected of him he naturally became worse. Margaret cast her eyes to heaven and reminded us of Martin's achievements at his age, the medal he won for Latin composition when he was twelve, the two scholarships at fifteen, his monotonous position at the head of his class always. Andrew listened sullenly – such topics were always raised in his presence. On one terrible occasion when they kept picking at his dead mother, he made a quiet protest and created a never-to-be-forgotten uproar. I remember the evening well, an overcast one in August with frequent drenching showers. Andrew had been forbidden to go out, and they had lit a dim fire up in the drawing-room around which we all sat while the wind rattled the windows. Ruth was reading her book in the corner. Martin was looking over some accounts for his mother. It was Hanny who glanced up from her sewing and began the old subject again.

'Tell us, Andrew, whatever did your mother do with that fine suit of clothes your father wore coming over the last summer we saw him?'

'I don't know, Aunt Hanny.'

'You must know. The light grey one. Did she give it to the local jumble sale? – and it very probably a Protestant jumble sale at that.'

'I don't know, Aunt Hanny.'

To my dismay, Margaret joined in. 'There were those lovely shoes too – remember them, Hanny? The two-tones and the fine black patent. They'd have done Martin nicely and he with the same little feet.'

'That's enough, Mother,' Martin said quietly, in a warning tone, looking at Andrew wriggling in his chair.

'How is it enough when those clothes belonged by rights to Alex's family – to us? Can you not remember what happened to them, Andrew?'

'Mother!' said Martin once more, and when she smiled, affecting not to understand, Martin slammed the cash-book shut and walked across the room, followed by Ruth who looked very pale.

'Come out for a walk with us, Andrew?' she smiled, placing a hand on his shoulder as she passed his chair, and when the boy got thankfully up to follow her, Eleanor looked up from a fashion magazine she was leafing through.

'Sorry, Ruth,' she said, 'he hasn't done the jobs I gave him after lunch. Wait until you're given leave to go, Andrew.'

'We'll be on the cliff road if it's not raining,' Ruth murmured to the boy as she left the room, and that was one of the occasions when I ought to have asserted myself. I ought to have told Eleanor I'd do whatever jobs the boy had neglected. I ought to have defied her and told Andrew to go. There are, after all, limits. An obscene squabble over a dead man's clothes which by ancient rural right belong to his family was no thing to submit a child to, when the man happens to be his father. But for so long I've beaten down my own resistance to such scenes that I doubt if I could have found the simple words to release the boy. But I didn't try. I didn't try. I am certainly to blame for the disgraceful scene which followed.

'Try and remember, Andrew,' Eleanor said carelessly turning over a page. 'Did Janet have a friend at that time who might have taken a fancy to the good grey suit?'

'I don't know, Ma'am.'

'She might have had two or three friends for all we know,' Hanny joined in eagerly. 'She was a forward lassie I always thought, but sure what could you expect from a pig but a grunt.'

I stood up. 'We'll go for a walk, son, now that the rain's over, and I'll help you with the chores later.'

'You can't have heard me, Con. I said he was not to go out until he has done the kitchen jobs.'

She was defying me now, and smiling lazily with great charm at the same time. I glanced from her to her two sisters and noted the same exclusive look on their very different faces. The invisible battle lines were drawn between the O'Donohues and the rest of us. Eleanor might never have gone away, never have qualified in London, never have lived a life of her own for so long, with me, thousands of miles away from this room. I walked weakly over to the window, laying my hand on Andrew's head for a moment as I passed him in his chair, shocked eyes at bay. Outside the window a spill of sulphury light fell from torn black clouds to melt in a track along the water. Make them stop it. Just make them stop.

But they went on. They went on to remember a Morocco leather suitcase which Eleanor had given her brother to which Janet and worse still Janet's family could have no possible right. When had he last seen that? Was it at his English grandmother's house? What about Alex's gold pocket watch, the one Mother had had inscribed for him when he came of age? That should have been put in the bank for Andrew when he grew up – where was that? And there was the engraved silver cigarette case . . .

'Long since sold to strangers,' Hanny said fiercely, 'and the money squandered by Janet on God knows what foolishness.'

'Were you ever told about possessions of your father's that would be yours when you grew up?' Margaret said, not unkindly if you didn't remember all that had gone before.

'No, Aunt Margaret.'

'There might be papers somewhere,' Eleanor said

thoughtfully. 'They should probably have been handed over with Andrew himself. I must contact the solicitor again some time.'

'What papers?' Hanny said contemptuously. 'Wouldn't every last pin of any value have been handed over to her people, whatever ragtag and bobtail sort they may have been? We don't know the half of what poor Alex let himself in for when he got mixed up with that lot.'

Andrew stood up, his wits gathered about him at last. 'Can I go now to do the jobs, Ma'am?'

'Very well, but be sure you clean out the oven properly,' Eleanor said. I thought Andrew would make himself scarce without further ado, but he went over to Hanny with some considerable dignity, blushing at the same time to the roots of his hair.

'My grandfather was a chemist in Canterbury,' Andrew said, 'my grandmother was a schoolteacher like Aunt Margaret. If they were alive 'tis with them I'd be living now, and glad to be out of this house.'

He was about to go, leaving Hanny with mouth open in shock, when Eleanor sprang quickly at him from her corner and smacked him quickly three times across the face with her open hand. The force from her considerable height tilted him sideways and I took action at last, holding him shaking in my arms.

'Shame on you, Eleanor! One would have thought

you'd be the one to defend your son from the vicious attacks made on him and his people, about whom we know little and nothing whatever to their discredit. Go, please, Andrew, and I'll see you downstairs. I'd just like to say this before I go myself. If what I've heard here this afternoon is Christianity, I'm sorry I didn't join the ranks of Islam while I was posted in the Middle East.'

Eleanor was laughing as I closed the door, but at least it would be something to quote to Ruth when she tackled me as I knew she would. We were walking out by the headland beyond the old town walls, as I said, under a sky washed clean by the rain. There was still an hour or so of daylight. Why, Ruth wanted to know. Why?

'It's a long story, Ruth.'

'When people say that they never want to tell you,' Ruth said, 'but you must defend him because he has nobody else. Adoption means thinking of a child as your own and you don't. Neither does Eleanor.'

'Neither does Eleanor think of her own Julia that way.'

'Oh, Con.' She turned away from me, distressed beyond measure, and more than ever I wanted to reach out and touch her but kept my hands clenched in my pockets instead. Oh Ruth. I can't remember positively when she stopped being Martin's wife and became separate, an infinitely desirable young woman, but I think it was the day we had a drink together before lunch. That pleasant little interlude in the pub (for both of us, I think) was followed by one of those viciously traumatic scenes back in the house, and if Eleanor had only known it, maybe that time her uproar was justified. Maybe she did know it. Maybe she did know that after the best part of thirty years' rejection and acceptance of rejection, I was free, my body was liberated in its response to a girl who (of course) so far as age was concerned might have been my daughter. She was in fact a few years younger than Julia, but how different. How warm and free and happy. Beautiful? I don't think so. Eleanor was once beautiful. Even people whom she wounded admitted that. But Ruth had certainly the clear eyes of youth and health, a way of moving that suggested harmony with her surroundings, a way of smiling and a concentration that probably everybody who talks to her believes is reserved for himself, and she has too an understanding of human misery and a response to it that are I think unusual in one so young. All this is rationalisation of course.

For me she has in addition a strong sensual pull that draws me to imagine her constantly in surroundings that are none of my business. I imagine her roused by perhaps a random touch of Martin's and rising like a fish to it. I hear her laugh, if he is unaware, I see her deliberately touch him in return, again and again, if he is tired or abstracted, but of course I do not see his eventual response although I know it always happens. What I see is her triumphant body at its moment of appeasement, I hear her quickly indrawn breath, then again I hear her laugh, her puppy nuzzlings, the fleshly jokes familiar yet always funny and always desired. I do not ever see her changing her mind, withdrawing what was clearly offered, becoming abstracted or bored or cruelly determined to withhold her own pleasure for savouring later and alone. I don't see any, in short, of the female routines I became familiar with over a period of fifteen years or more until at last all carnal response in me died suddenly and (I had thought) for ever. Even as a young fellow whores had never particularly appealed to me. Abroad, I've left them more often than not after paying for what I didn't bother to take. That was long ago.

In recent years celibacy has had its positive tidy appeal. Because Eleanor has always refused to live in Dublin, I rented a flat for years close to the British Embassy, ever since the war made postings abroad improbable. For the first couple of years I lived with a young translator who worked for us at that time but when she returned to London I didn't try to replace her. It seemed more trouble than it was worth, which meant I suppose that old age had arrived at last. I thought the habit of celibacy had come to stay until Ruth came down with Martin that first summer and I watched as in the theatre that sensual unfolding again. I don't think they ever touched one another publicly with passion. It was something understood, there like a drumbeat one waits for because it's in the score. But I thought it had nothing to do with me, that I could enjoy it as one enjoys an unspoken joke familiar to everybody. The old house seemed enriched by them, it seemed to gather them in. Ruth was so sure of herself and of her hold on life that not even the three sisters could shake her confidence, although in the beginning I saw them trying, especially of course Hanny.

Eleanor, once Ruth had been tried and found adequate, actually grew fond of her and, I could see, often sought her company. Martin had always been a favourite of hers and Eleanor seemed particularly happy that he had chosen well. Hanny, after ignoring Ruth for a while, began to regard her more or less in the same light as Martin despite what she thought of as the bad and sinful start to their marriage. Margaret, his mother, was happy from the moment she discovered Ruth was 'nice', as she put it, a nice responsible girl obviously from a good family.

Naturally when the twins were born Ruth was regarded as having paid up her life subscription in the family. She was one of them. Her sons could not fail to be clever and in due course add to the stock of certificates upstairs. All was as it should be.

But now? You can successfully ignore a situation only so long as you do not put words on it. The very laws of diplomacy enshrine the substitution of acceptable phrases in place of the truth. The moment I betray verbally a suspicion of my feeling for Ruth is the moment when I can no longer enjoy it, however fearfully. A fragile situation will fall instantly apart, and then I will have nothing. No faint excitement on awakening that never used to be there. No gradual image forming behind closed eyelids of Ruth standing at the window to savour another day. No sensual stake in the world other people take for granted. A rather contemptibly selfish attitude. What of Ruth?

What of her? She was happy, although disturbed occasionally by the misery of others. If she could know that I warmed myself at somebody else's fire I don't think she would have minded, but I couldn't be sure. In her eyes I was naturally an old man. Strong sexual feeling in one of my age might have seemed to her slightly obscene anyway, but directed at herself it could only be reprehensible. So one had to be cautious. Guard above all the eyes behind sunglasses in case she could read their joy in every movement she made. She was pleading now for Andrew and for Julia too, and what could one say? I will belatedly love them or go through the motions of loving them for your sake? I will take Andrew to the orthodontist who will straighten his teeth but who can do nothing for his wounded spirit. I will perhaps take Julia to Cork and buy her baggy corduroys and a nice shirt in which she will look her age and maybe feel better, but I cannot love her. Even for you, Ruth. Even for you.

'So will you, Con? Promise?'

'I can't promise – it mightn't be possible – but I'll try to think myself inside their heads and I'll try to cushion them. More I can't promise.'

'That will be enough.' She was smiling now. She took my arm and tightened her fingers on it and I had to walk on beside her with head bent, hands in my pockets.

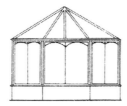

When I was a child we moved around a lot in the early days but Ferrycarrig was the anchor. We went there for six weeks or more every summer and it never changed. You picked up old friends again as easily as you found your fishing rod in the exact corner of the back hall where you'd left it last holidays. Once I even found a tin of old lug worms, though it took me quite a while to work out what the mummified remains had originally been. Home was always changing, even in the days when my father still taught school. He would stay as long as he still had a hope of becoming Principal, at most three years or so, and then we would move on to the next small school whose ad. he had read over breakfast and which had held out a prospect of advancement. He was never promoted, not because he wasn't a good teacher but because he wouldn't take control. There was frequently uproar in his classes while he patiently explained some problem or other to some slow pupil. The others would go wild, and though at that time when beating children at school was practised by virtually every schoolteacher, my father didn't believe in it. He was gentle and people walked over him. He moved on to the next school and so did we.

It was useless arranging your room the way you liked it, building bookshelves or anything of that kind. You knew you'd be packing up again almost before you'd finished settling in. But Ferrycarrig remained.

My room there was at the top of the house, with two dormers overlooking the harbour and inside all the possessions I had gathered about me since the age of three or so in this house: nice shells, chunks of rock, airplanes (suspended from the ceiling) constructed from kits people gave me as presents, toy boats, books of course, a dried starfish hanging between the curtains, games Dad bought us to while away rainy August afternoons. Ferrycarrig provided all the continuity we never found at home.

It was better of course after he gave up formal teaching and Mother became Principal of a primary school in Cork. After that we lived in the same house for all of ten years, which Dad helped to run in between coaching maths to backward pupils. The small sitting-room was given over to his books and papers. Sometimes pupils came to him and sometimes he went to them – that was usually up to the big houses in Montenotte where parlourmaids in brown dresses and frilled aprons served him tea on a silver tray. It suited him better than the hurly burly of the classroom but it paid very little. It was Mother who kept the house going, who paid most of the bills. Dad was always good for a handsome fountain pen if exams were coming up, for a new fishing rod in the summer, for a few bob to go to the pictures. My sister (much older than I) and two older brothers left home early on University scholarships and for several years I was the only one at home. I learned to know my father rather well, and he was not unhappy, nor I believe was he ever made to feel inadequate by my mother. That happened later when she retired and they could no longer cope with the expense of renting the house in Cork. They came to live in Ferrycarrig, where of course my widowed grandmother was always ready to welcome anybody who saw the light and came home again. Mother I think quickly settled back into the life of her old home, but my father was destroyed by it. It's a big word, but I think he was.

It happened little by little. One day I remember he brought home a pot of blackcurrant jam from the town, just took it out of his pocket and laid it with a smile on the tea table as he might at home. There was an instant inquisition. Where had he bought it? What had he paid for it? Shop jam was a cruel waste of money and not even good to eat either. My father bent his head and waited until the storm passed. Then Hanny got up from the table and said to him, 'Come till I show you, James, why you're never to do that again.'

She led him down a stone passage to the larder and there she showed him why he must never do that again. There were two shelves of chutney and three of neatly labelled jam pots. There were bottled pears on the lowest shelf and above them a shelf of marmalade made in January. All of this had been done by Hanny the provider, who fed and nourished everybody when she felt like it and retired to bed when she did not. She was visited now and again by a strange malaise, which necessitated drawn curtains and no food for several days. But now she stood there smiling triumphantly I have no doubt at silly James, showing him the notes pencilled on faded paper stuck to the back of the larder door:

July 1917: 130 lbs strawberry
August 1917: 70 lbs crab apple jelly
September 1917: 50 lbs blackberry & apple

The faint scrawl was in old Julia's hand, and Hanny laughed as she showed it to my father. 'I could hardly do less than carry on now that Mama is beyond it, could I, James?' He told me the whole story months afterwards, by which time he could smile at it.

My father never showed any signs ever of hurt, but my mother could read him like a book. I remember he told me her exact words. 'That's the nicest jam I've tasted for a long time in this house – with all the jam that's made here, you never see so much as a spoonful of blackcurrant. Have some, Hanny.'

Hanny said thank you but she never liked to let shop jam pass her lips – you never knew what rubbish was in it. I spooned some onto my brown bread and joined Mother in praising my father's choice. He smiled and said nothing. I noticed he didn't taste the jam himself and that he only drank one cup of tea.

It wasn't I suppose a very important defeat, his effort to contribute something he bought himself to this house, but my father was easily discouraged. It was a long time before he tried again, and then the result was much the same. My cousin Julia had torn an old threadbare roller towel on the back of the scullery door and had got into trouble for it. Dad arrived back from his walk with two new roller towels which he presented to Hanny. She thanked him politely, and later we heard her sewing machine working away noisily in the front room. She appeared with two sewn-up replacement towels made from a threadbare bath sheet and one of these was fitted behind the scullery door. My father's offerings were never seen again. Somebody stripping this house for auction at some future date that must come will find them among the masses of unused linen in the big chest upstairs.

Meanwhile my mother said, 'That was very thoughtful of you, James,' but anybody could see that Dad was finding it heavy going after only two years in this house.

Quite simply, he had nothing to do. In Cork he had his routines, certain days when people came to him for grinds, certain other days when he went to pupils' houses. He coached English and Maths (a curious combination) for University entrance and Leaving Cert, he was painstaking, kind to boneheads, and quick to develop natural ability. He produced results. On his way home from somebody's house he would also pick up certain agreed items of shopping for my mother but he would also remember that one of us needed an extra coathook in his room or a bookshelf or a bottle of Stephens' Blue Ink or a copy of some out-of-print book or even some medicament for a sore throat. He would always remember these things. It was a delight to come in and unexpectedly find that your room had its extra bookshelf, that every last wood-shaving had been cleared away and that the shelf had already been given its first coat of paint. Everybody in our family appreciated these things, exclaimed over them. We had been trained by my mother from an early age never to take them for granted. They were the sort of things she never had time for herself. They were the sort of things that made our house different from the others we knew where both parents worked. When in the course of time the girl who came to clean the house took a job in Dublin and was difficult to replace at a wage we could afford, my father took to hoovering floors and polishing brasses as well. You never saw him doing these things, but you noticed that they were done. What you did notice my father doing was taking it easy, reading, filling his pipe, strolling to the pub at the other end of the road where he had a single pint every night and turned over the day's news with a few cronies. Every Wednesday he went to the cinema with Mother.

If I ever knew a happy man, I think it was my father. He had time to listen to people. Very often he didn't say much, but you saw a problem in a new light when you talked to him. He was easy in his own mind, had been unhappy (as Mother told me once) only when he was in a competitive situation. He didn't like scoring. He failed as a professional schoolmaster because he was unwilling to take his share of authority. Authority? The word meant nothing to him. Even when we were children he never said we must do this or that, must not do something else. He would consider the matter for a moment and say something like, 'I shouldn't do that if I were you because . . .' Because his voice was so quiet, you listened to him. As often as not you did as he seemed to be suggesting. It is a mode of governing that only works on a one to one basis. He ended up with a family which never felt harried. To this day the easy relationships he built up among us hold good. We enjoy one another's company, see one another whenever we can. I have a bed whenever I want it from my brother in Paris, my sisters in London. Likewise they know I welcome them at any time. We like to keep track of one another. Sometimes I am trying to get through to my brother at the same time as he is dialling my number. I think if my father could know he would be happy. Above all things in life he hated quarrelling.

Why, I wonder, whatever the financial pressures, did they ever retire to Ferrycarrig? It was a summer house, beautiful to remember because of the big windows and the harbour and the green hills on the other side. When you thought about it and the town in winter, you didn't remember the pressures of that house. You remembered the town's slow pace of life, its capacity to absorb hundreds of summer visitors and remain itself. You remembered above all that in the household old Maurice made nothing ever changed. One summer melted into another without trace. It was a summer house.

But after my parents retired there I could see how

it changed my father. He hadn't realised that he held his share of control with my mother at home, but in Ferrycarrig it would always be different. She was not in control there herself and, above all, she slipped very easily back into being one of the three sisters who might quarrel among themselves but tended to close ranks when challenged from outside. I could see her actually becoming a different person when Ferrycarrig was her home again.

Of course it happened gradually, but I think for my father the change was more brutal. Quite simply he wasn't needed, and he had no structures on which to rebuild his life. He belonged to the generation that thought leisure had to be 'earned'. You earned it by putting in a considerable amount of work every day, and that done, you could enjoy your leisure. I remember pointing out to him once that there were whole areas of the river up country from the estuary that he didn't know.

He didn't have a car, but when I was down one spring by myself I first suggested a fishing trip for the two of us and then, because I knew he had spent most of his life alone and might prefer it, I suggested leaving him and his tackle bag at one of my own favourite reaches of the river and collecting him two or three hours later. We could have a pint on the way home. First he said yes and then he made excuses. The weather broke on the second day and he said better leave it until I was down in the summer.

What in fact, I often wonder now, did he do with his day in Ferrycarrig? I tried once or twice to puzzle it out. He was always up early, as long as I've known him. At weekends you might have found my mother in her dressing gown at eleven o'clock, but never him. He liked, as Ruth does, to sample the morning. Shaved and dressed, you would sometimes find him in the garden staring around him. He might say, 'Next year I think I'll put a hydrangea in that corner,' but he often forgot when the right planting time came along. He would much more likely ask you to observe the particular construction of a spider's web, showing you with his fingers how it differed from one in the far corner, wondering if different sorts of spider constructed different webs or if the web any particular spider made at a particular time depended on the season or the weather or a passing whim. Next day he might have a book on spiders out from the library and regale us in the evening with details of courtship and the peculiar difficulty female spiders have in deciding whether a male is a mate or a meal. After mating (if it happens) it seems the male has to make his escape pretty sharp. I know this and hundreds of other fascinations because of my father who died – from lack of interest – five years after he retired to Ferrycarrig.

What did he do with his days there? Sometimes I think the question haunts me. If only he had lived long enough for his twin grandsons to have whiled away long summer days with him listening to the life cycle of insects or shellfish, learning to know him in such a way that they would remember him for the rest of their lives as I do. They were only three when he died, babies who cried easily and hadn't yet learned to listen. I know of course that one of the things he did with his days was pore over mail-order catalogues. I found a dozen or more in his room, many items marked with a neat black star. Were these what he hoped eventually to order, having already acquired some of them? A pressure cooker, for instance, which Hanny never used, a set of handsomely designed chessmen but made of plastic (my mother could never learn to play though sometimes Con played with him), a watch which purported to tell the date and year and which seldom worked properly, two sets of thermal underwear which were untouched in his drawer when he died, a fishing anorak for the trips he never took, a leather-bound Izaak Walton which I still have. I know he made plans sometimes because I kept one letter from him.

Dear Martin,
Glad to hear you and Ruth are doing well and that the twins have acquired a tooth each.

Maybe I might come up on the train to see you all for Hallow Eve as you kindly suggest, but to tell you the truth it's been a very bad couple of months down here and I had this daft idea of taking your mother away to the sun as a surprise for the anniversary. I've got a few brochures from the travel agents and the cost seems reasonable. A few dividends I'd almost forgotten about came in and I think we could manage it for a week or ten days. Malaga seems to be the nearest place where sun can be guaranteed this time of the year, but I wouldn't like the look of those big high hotels and I don't think your mother would either. Of course they are very usual everywhere nowadays. I thought maybe the Canary Islands – only a little more expensive – might be less developed and one might be able to make it clear to the travel agent that what we have in mind is a nice little hotel.

All here are well and send love. Con and Eleanor and the children say they will come down for lunch on Sunday.

My love to you all, Dad.

I sent him a whole folderful of brochures about reasonable places in the sun, about end-of-season bargains particularly in Greece which all his life I knew he had wanted to see. He could quote you all of that Byron poem about the isles of Greece where burning Sappho loved and sang. The idea that he might go there fascinated me and I phoned my brother in Paris who said he had been trying for years to make them visit him. If they were going to Greece they could surely stop off at Paris and extend their holiday a bit, couldn't they?

I knew it was intended as a surprise for my mother so I couldn't mention it to her but kept up as much pressure as I could on the old man. There was a long silence. Hallow Eve came and went. Then I got a letter to say plans had been changed and they were coming to spend a few days in the Royal Marine Hotel in Dun Laoire. We persuaded them to come and spend an extra week with us, which they did. We got a babysitter in and took them a couple of nights to the theatre and a couple of nights out to dinner. My mother politely tried to conceal the fact that she couldn't wait to get back to Ferrycarrig. When I asked him about the Canary Islands and the Isles of Greece he just smiled with embarrassment like a child caught playacting in front of a mirror, and said it was a daft idea anyway these hard times, wasn't it? Then I knew the three sisters had taken a united stand against the trip and that was that. I found the travel brochures all carefully labelled and in separate big envelopes after he died. I also found the Blue Guide to Crete and a translation of the Odyssey.

What I remember directly about his life in Ferrycarrig stems from a couple of visits I made there by myself in the off season. At that time I ran a highly temperamental motorbike which frequently landed me in trouble on the road. So I seldom told them in advance that I was coming down in case I might have to spend the weekend dismantling an engine on the side of the road. I therefore fancy that I found them (when I did make it) more or less as they normally were. Everybody puts on a show of some kind when he knows he is going to be on view – it takes different people in different ways, even inside the same family. My mother, for instance, polishes the hall table, curls her hair, and never leaves the front window.

My father would spend an hour or so just looking around the visitor's room to see what he might add to it. He tended to hang around the house, open the front door, sometimes even take a stroll to the corner, and he liked to be the first to announce that somebody was coming. Hanny bakes a tea brack, buys porksteak, and puts out the cat.

There is always this air of relief about the house when you arrive. They can then get on with whatever it is they might have been doing. If you come unexpectedly they always say, 'Be sure to let us know next time,' and they point out how much better your weekend could have been if they'd known.

Anyhow I arrived one squally Sunday in March, having broken down the previous day on the road and spent the night in a Youth Hostel. The tension in the house when I walked in could have been cut with a blunt knife. Eleanor and Con and the children were down for the day, and Julia was in floods of tears in the kitchen, being scolded as though she were a child by Hanny. Up in the drawing-room Eleanor sat with face averted from Con and my mother was clearly attempting to make peace between them. Old Julia alone sat imperviously in her wheelchair, busy with a piece of linen. She greeted me kindly, calling me Alex – a son who had been dead for many years. Andrew it seems had disappeared without permission, without even unpacking the offerings cooked by Eleanor and brought down in the boot of the car. They attempted to greet me cheerfully, as though they had just been surprised at a game of Happy Families, but it wasn't very successful. I soon escaped to look for my father. I'd been told he was 'out'.

He was out in a cutting March wind with no overcoat on and he had taken refuge from a shower of hail in one of the bathing shelters along the promenade, a pretty Victorian affair with fretted ironwork forming a domed roof and letting in the east wind. He was sitting facing the churned up sea with an expression of desolation on his face that I have never forgotten, but which vanished immediately as he rose to greet me.

'I sat down here to watch the herring gulls at their diving – look over there, son!'

But he hadn't been looking in the direction of the herring gulls when I saw him. He hadn't been reading his newspaper or filling his pipe. He had been staring at a cold sea with his miserable eyes and I guessed by the chill of his hands that he had been there a long time. When I asked him why he wasn't wearing his overcoat he said he had just run out to find Andrew who had the key of the car and was supposed to have locked it up again after unpacking.

'Come to Hogans and I'll buy you a hot whisky,' I said, 'Andrew has probably long since unpacked and gone out again.'

He shrugged and with what I can only describe as the impish expression of a child escaping punishment because a visitor has intervened, he stumped off with me to the hotel, the only place open at four o'clock of a Sunday afternoon. Never had anywhere seemed more welcoming.

There was a big fire in the lounge, and although the bar was closed they would always bring you a whisky with coffee.

On a sudden bright impulse I ordered Irish coffee for both of us, and my father chuckled delightedly as he spooned extra dark brown sugar into his.

'Warm the cockles of your heart,' he said and we sipped in perfect silent companionship until our glasses were half empty. Then he sat back and started to fill his pipe. I lit a cigarette.

'Warmer now?'

'As a bug in a rug,' he said. He drew slowly on his pipe and asked me about Dublin, my studies, and (as always) was I looking after myself well on the scholarship money. Was I sure it was enough? I reminded him about my part-time job in the canteen and he seemed satisfied. Then he said something so odd that I've never forgotten.

'Remember, son, never be short of money.'

'You sound like Polonius.'

'A sensible old man, Polonius. Neither a borrower nor a lender be – lucky the man who is neither, I tell you. But if you ever lack money for any particular piece of nonsense, let me know. There are times when a little money to squander may be the saving of a man's self-respect and the lack of it may cost him a lot more than the extravagance. Remember that.'

'How are you yourself?'

He knew what I was asking him. He didn't answer at once and then he shrugged. 'You miss old routines until you've established new ones.'

'But you've been here three years now.'

'I was ten years in the same house in Cork, don't

forget that. And of course you were all young. There was plenty to do.'

'Did you ever think of finding pupils here?'

'Hanny says they don't go in for that sort of thing in this town – the only people who ever do grinds are local students who commute to Cork. They'd think it very odd if a man of my age went looking for private pupils.'

'You never know until you try. You're likely to be a lot more patient and experienced than any student.'

'We'll see,' he said, 'we'll see,' but I knew he wouldn't. I could nearly hear Hanny's speeches. 'You'd be as well known as a begging ass trying to take the bite out of a young student's mouth. You'd make a laughing stock of yourself and of this whole house!'

He didn't need to tell me any of this. It was only too obvious. He let me pay for the coffee in an obvious desire not to offend me, but when I was leaving early next morning to be in time for a two o'clock lecture he slipped me a tenner and said it was interest that he didn't need on a little Post Office savings account.

Never be short of money. The curious thing is that he never was – quite. When he died, after having bought me a new motorbike only six months previously, he left one hundred and eighty-five pounds in his Post Office book, a balance of sixteen pounds at the Bank, and three Prize Bonds. He had, of course, a paid-up insurance policy to cover the funeral expenses, and it was the sort of tidy pull-out he must have striven to make. It would be an over-simplification to say he had lived a wasted life. He didn't look at it that way. Ferrycarrig was obviously a mistake, but otherwise his life had been useful to many hundreds of people, and he had enjoyed it. Even long after his death, he was never known in Cork as anything but 'The Master'. In a pub there one night an unknown man came up and shook me warmly by the hand. 'You'd be the Master's son, God be good to him? Only for himself and his help with the Maths I'd be out of a job like the rest of them, instead of being cushy enough in the Corporation. What will you have, boy?' It wasn't a bad requiem. He'd have been delighted to hear his memory had earned me a drink from an old pupil.

After his death my mother went a little further adrift from Dad's safe anchorage and reverted totally to being an O'Donohue again. She now thought as a corporate entity with them, and Con in his turn (when eventually they came down to live here) became the outsider. Con however was a native of the town. He had local sources of friendship if he cared to call on them and of course he knew his way around people's past history. He was never made to feel an outsider in the town, as I think my father was. One of the great tragedies for me was that my father never knew Ruth very well because in the early days she was always busy with the babies. As

I said he died when they were three. It is their loss as well as his that he never knew them well. He was a nice man. They would never have forgotten him if they had once known him.

That however is, as they say, water under the bridge. Margaret, my mother, remains and is fond of the family in her fashion – probably very fond of the children. They already chatter constantly about Ferrycarrig while they are in Dublin. It is somewhere warmly there in the back of their minds as it was in mine. It means summer and happy idleness to them. And to Ruth?

I never quite know, although we are open with one another about most things. Reared in a casual friendly way herself by parents who were both doctors, she has always found the 'scenes' which blow up every so often in that house baffling and difficult. City born, she doesn't know anything about the atavistic tensions of a country town where practically everybody is only a move or two away from peasant origins and privilege is fiercely guarded. Old Maurice, Founder of the Feast, so to speak, was a barefoot petticoated boy in the fields of West Cork, the brightest of his large family, sent away to school by an uncle who was a priest. He climbed through Local Government to end as County Manager and he set up his family in some style as evidenced by the house. Even the other house in Market Street where most of that family except Eleanor were reared, was solidly middle-class, although neither in location nor detail as handsome as Ferrycarrig. He achieved that beautiful old house just in time to die in it, and I think all his family have been very consciously living up to it ever since.

It was never considered by old Julia that any of them married with sufficient care. Each of them to a greater or lesser extent married down and the runners-in like Con and my own father (to mention only those considered the best of them) were always made to feel this. Probably the only thing that would have been entirely acceptable to the O'Donohues was old money, established position in that little peninsula beyond the town where there were a few large and beautiful estates that sent their young across the water for education and marriage partners. Eleanor might have been expected to catch one of them (or somebody of equal value) since she was beautiful, doing well in a respected profession, and always so sure of herself. It didn't happen, and Con was made to suffer for it even although he had reached the highest diplomatic rank in his own profession.

All of this Ruth found it impossible to understand, although I think she liked the three sisters individually. It was the atmosphere they combined to create that she found, I fear, oppressive. I know she liked the town and I know she accepted that the boys had a right both to enjoy the place while they were small and to keep the memory of it as grown men. Her own parents had died in an air crash on their way to a medical conference so there was no continuity there. The boys never knew that set of grandparents and Ruth was an only child.

Looking back on it all now, I think I was wrong to urge her to spend so long there every summer. I think she really only enjoyed it for the two or three weeks when I could be there and, by the time I realised this, many summers had gone by. I'm not likely to forget the time when the scales finally fell from my eyes. It was that hot summer when the boys were eight. Even now I'm not entirely sure that I understand all the undercurrents of the situation.

It had been one of those rare brilliant summers up to the time when the boys got their summer holidays. There was no real need that year to urge Ruth to take them down to Ferrycarrig and stay there until early August when I would be free. She went off happily when school broke up in late June, and when she phoned me that night she seemed delighted with herself and the baked golden grass up on the sand dunes – evidence everywhere that the summer had already arrived (as it had also in town) and probably intended to stay. I had a long letter from her at the end of the second week and it made me happy to think of them enjoying themselves down there.

'Most afternoons,' she wrote, 'we take the ferry across to Derrybeg and pack a picnic. Hanny stays at home of course to take care of Eleanor and Gran, although Eleanor writes notes telling her not to bother. The rest of us including your mother go over with Julia and Andrew and the boys, bringing enough food to do an army. Con brings his fishing gear and your mother brings her sewing. We set up a kind of camp with windbreakers (unnecessary!) in the shade of the high wall from which most of us move out into the blasting sun. Already the boys and I and Andrew and Con are dark brown from swimming and being blazed on while our skin is salty. Whenever it gets too hot we just flop back into the water again. Would you believe it that Con has taken to swimming too? – first time in about fifteen years, your mother says. He swims well, and has taught the boys to crawl. Sometimes he challenges me to race him but I always lose.'

One day I gather he couldn't resist showing off – an old man's trick while he is still sound of wind and limb. He got on to what we used to call 'the railway' when we were kids, and he drifted fast out of sight around the small headland to the west of Derrybeg. I have no doubt Con first went on 'the railway' around the beginning of the First World War when he would have been home on school holidays. 'The railway' is the fear and despair of those parents who know of it – fortunately, mine didn't, nor probably did Con's mother since in his day women aged young and wouldn't have dreamed of going swimming. Most of that generation couldn't swim anyway and heartily feared the water. 'The railway' is a strong current which runs diagonally between the harbour and the mouth of the estuary some two miles away. If you use it properly and let yourself go it can carry you fast and effortlessly up to the wooded estuary. There you can go ashore, cross a bridge, and make the return journey on another current going in the opposite direction – or back, more or less, to where you began. It could be highly dangerous to those who got caught by accident, but if you knew what you were doing (and generations of town boys did) it was probably the nearest thing to the thrill of perpetual motion without effort that you were ever likely to encounter. As I read the letter in which Ruth described 'the railway', I thought I could get inside old Con's mind as I imagined the scene. This was, in effect, a magical return to boyhood. This was a way to defy old age as one hot bright day followed another and the water was warm enough not to bother old bones. I fancied it was even a harmless showing off before Ruth, whom I knew he liked and who liked him.

One day when the boys were occupied with Andrew building a moat for their castle and Julia helping them, Ruth on some impulse that came no doubt from the careless summer itself, decided to go on 'the railway' herself. Had I been there I'd have stopped her. Had I been there I'd have been, no doubt, as nervous as I'd be about the boys. But it seems she swam out to the steely blue rumpled stretch of water before Con realised what she was doing and then his only course (as it would have been mine) was to follow her.

Ruth is no coward, but the first time you get on the railway it is terrifying. You don't believe you will be swept inland and you don't believe you will ever be in control of your direction again. If you struggle you can get into real trouble, you can tire yourself out and be drowned. I'm not sure, but I gather Ruth at some stage started to do something of the sort and Con, some hundred yards or so behind, shouted to her to lie still on the water – 'float and look at the sky' are the words she remembers. She obeyed, and she doesn't know how long she floated on the strong irresistible current. She remembers the town being lost in the distance, she remembers the heat of the sun on her face. She remembers being afraid at one stage of falling asleep and she remembers saying to herself, This is how it happens, death happens like this. It's easy. Children are still making sandcastles, people are still lying in the sun, and nobody knows. But Con, of course, knew. She told me she was not at the time sure whether she had heard his voice telling her to float or whether she had imagined it. What she remembers quite positively is believing she would never see me again. She said she imagined my face when the local Garda Sergeant came to the door to say she had been drowned.

What she remembers next is a rattle of pebbles and suddenly being able to find her feet again, so suddenly that she thought she was dreaming. The town seemed very far away in a blue haze and nearby were willows trailing into the water and tall meadowsweet and buttercups. She was at the mouth of the great salmon river and there was nothing to stop her clambering out onto the banks and getting herself together. But she remembers losing hold once again and being gripped strongly in somebody's arms, being carried to where there was soft long damp grass which bent in the breeze and tickled her face.

She remembers laughing and then nothing more until she awakened to Con's gentle slapping of her face and her cold hands. When she opened her eyes the tears were pouring down his face, she remembers, and he said, 'You must never do that again – never never again, promise me!' as he would to a child.

Somebody he knew drove them back (sitting on folded newspapers to save the seats) and Hanny was horrified (I can imagine) and said they were disgracing the house. Con went up to get dressed and suggested Ruth should take a bath and go to bed, but she was dressed as soon as he was and determined to go back over on the ferry with him in case the boys were missing her and frightened. In fact the sandcastle (which by now had a deep moat gradually filling up with water) had occupied all their attention – they hadn't even noticed she was not still swimming in the harbour. Julia was lying on her face unconcernedly and my mother was also reading, sitting in the black shadow of the wall which bordered a ruined estate. It was as if nothing had happened, yet I knew when I went down the following week that what had happened was somehow significant to Ruth. Maybe she had, maybe we had, taken happiness for granted. I knew when I touched her it was not like that any more. It was as if she, not I, had come home from a very long journey and the mere fact of being in my arms was some sort of miracle. That night I knew that even deep sensual peace such as ours has its islands and that the shores we reached that night had never been sighted before by her or by me. One other thing I remember. On the edges of sleep I was conscious of footsteps in the room below and noises I couldn't place for a moment. Then I remembered. Con was letting down the back rest on Eleanor's bed before settling her down for another unresigned night. I heard her beating with one hand on the springs, perhaps ordering him away now that she no longer had words to do it. Ruth whispered against my ear, 'We have too much – does it never worry you?' and I closed my hand over her mouth and then opened her lips again with one finger. The Town Hall clock struck midnight as we began to make love all over again to prove to her that it never worries me.

Next morning I went early to see Eleanor. I could never get used to her like this, chained to the small childish bed by the refusal of her muscles to do their work. I could never get used to the ruined mask-like face except when she turned the eyes full on me as she did that morning, Eleanor's eyes in a wrecked body which belonged to somebody else.

'How are you?' When I kissed her I knew she did not refuse it, that was all. She couldn't smile but the eyes warmed a little and the hand that could move – the left one – felt alive in my own. I told her about Ruth, whom I had left fast asleep in her bed upstairs, a sign of how exhausted she was. I told her about 'the railway' when we were children, which she very likely didn't know about. It was boys rather than girls who played that particular game of chance. Eleanor's good hand lay quietly in mine as I told her about my own railway experiences, and the time Dan McNally's father went after him in a boat and beat the lard out of him when he got him safely aboard.

All the time I talked I remembered how she was when I was a child, not only lovely to look at and apparently ageless but also (to me at least) invariably kind, the donor of unexpected gifts of money (though by reputation she was, in the local phrase, tight as tuppence), the interceder when I was in trouble over some holiday folly. Others might get the edge of her tongue, her daughter Julia might indeed have a hard time of it, but I (like Ruth after me) would accompany her on trips to King's, to town, to be given a new pair of shoes or maybe a box camera, maybe even accompany her to the cinema when her own children were confined to barracks for some crime. Often I didn't feel too good about it, but my mother always urged me not to refuse. Eleanor as the spoiled baby of that family had always done as she pleased and she had elected to spoil me. I must put up with it, which of course (put that way) it was a pleasure to do.

A shaft of yellow sun struck into her eyes as I went on trying to entertain her and my voice when I looked at her helplessness trailed away. If nobody came, she might have to spend an hour spotlighted by the burning sun simply because there was no way she could move. I went to draw enough of the curtain to close out the sun until it moved to a more acceptable position and as I did I suddenly couldn't stand the pretence any more. I fetched her notepad and wrote – to put us on equal terms – 'I've never admired the courage of a human being as I admire yours, Eleanor, for accepting this,' and while I held the pad she made with her left hand and the pencil I placed in it the faint spidery marks which added up to this:

'I DON'T accept it, you fool.'

'But,' I said, bending to take her small shoulders between the palms of my hands, 'you're here. You don't beat us away. You allow us to talk nonsense to you. You are . . .' I searched among all the childhood lumber for the phrase we used to use satirically but with a kind of admiration too. I found it. 'You are a Little Soldier.' A flicker of amusement appeared in her eyes but was instantly replaced by starkness. She felt again for the pencil and again I put it between her fingers and held the pad. I was on my knees beside the bed.

'I do not accept anything, Martin. I hate and defy God for doing it. Hate him.'

I noticed there was no capital H. It was very hard to answer her.

'Look, Eleanor, it wouldn't be natural if you didn't.' At this point Con came smiling in at her door, carrying orange juice, but she gestured him furiously away with the front of her closed hand. Nothing could have been plainer, and he went. 'Listen, Eleanor. What I said first was sentimental and stupid. If you did accept all this it would probably mean there was no fight left in you and you couldn't recover. I know now that inside of you there's the old Eleanor absolutely intact and I know you will recover.' When I said this she lowered her magnificent eyes and I saw the tears sliding down her face. 'Don't cry, Eleanor. Con is bringing another specialist down from Limerick next week and this man has put dozens of stroke cases together again. I'm positive you're going to be yourself by next week – maybe long before.'

Eleanor painfully scrawled another sentence: 'Damn you, I am a doctor.'

My mother and Hanny fortunately came in to change her bed at this point and I lifted Eleanor onto an armchair in the corner. She weighed not so much as a cocker spaniel.

As I went on talking to her I saw out of the corner of my eye Hanny and my mother silently signalling to one another in horror over the defiance Eleanor had scrawled at the Almighty and I saw (but turned Eleanor away towards the window from the sight) Hanny quickly tearing at the page.

Such blasphemy would bring down God's anger on us all, was what she would have said if she had dared. But Hanny regarded Eleanor's rages even in her altered state with some respect. On an impulse and with the consent I could only guess at from Eleanor, I carried her gently to Ruth who was just waking up. The change of scene delighted her and it gave the family the idea of setting up Eleanor in the front dining room downstairs, from which she could watch the town going by. I was idiotically pleased that I brought this about by a random impulse.

The surgeon from Limerick came and went but Eleanor refused to take his advice and enter hospital. Instead she set up a sort of salon in the dining-room. People coming in and out of the house remembered her because she was on a chaise longue by the window and they usually put their heads in at her door. Unwelcome visitors Eleanor received with eyes still staring out at the harbour. Those she wanted to approach her found themselves marvelling at the sight of Eleanor's huge eyes moving in her rigid face to welcome them. Sometimes it seemed to me she ought to veil her face from the nose down like Arab women and then she would almost be the old Eleanor again. Hanny, unless she was coming to perform some necessary task of nursing, was usually not welcome. My mother and Ruth and I were welcome and so were our children. Her own Julia and Andrew visited her once a day, usually not for long, and usually in embarrassed silence, knowing her impatience with them. Con braved the hostile averted eyes every day and chattered to her about town events, always finding some amusing story to bring her. Terminating these visits was difficult. She had written to me on her pad one day, 'Get him out of here as quickly as you can.' When I was in the house I would interrupt them after fifteen minutes or so. I became adroit at finding reasons for Con to go elsewhere and eventually his own intelligence took over. I would sometimes meet him at the door on his way out.

So the four weeks of my holiday wore away. There was no change in Eleanor as brilliant day followed brilliant day, and then finally came the Regatta, the week we were leaving. The following week the boys were due back at school so Ferrycarrig would be emptying according to the annual ritual. This always gave an edge to the Regatta festivities, which anyhow had been going on in the town on the 28th of August every year since 1890.

Down in the kitchen, stuck to the sides of the summer-house, were photographs of past regattas, old Maurice as a young man in flannels and boater, old Julia as a thin girl in sprigged muslin, a sash around her waist with its two ends caught by the breeze and a ravishing smile for the cameraman which in due course she would pass on to Eleanor. Behind her was a pair of crossed oars, each held by a grinning brother, both of them long since dead, and above them all was the festive bunting this town had always strung up all over the place for the regatta. In another group of prize winners was the young Con, very handsome in a sailor suit, beaming under a peaked cap like the rest of the winning oarsmen. Peeping in at the corner of that picture was tiny Hanny in a high-necked summer blouse with her hair done up in two bunches, ribbons at her throat and a wicked smile on her small pointy face. The smile said she could tell you things about all these gallant oarsmen (if only she chose) that would be nothing to their credit, and no doubt she could.

On the morning of the Regatta the boats began to come in from all around the coast, from Cobh, Ballycotton, Courtmacsherry, Youghal, Kinsale and dozens of smaller places. Beflagged lifeboats carried crowds of chattering people who brought portable grandmothers, infants and toddlers by the hundred. Currachs followed the long sea roads from Dingle manned by tall silent men in navy blue ganseys who after their race would shut themselves away in a quayside pub and not be seen again until morning. The town as usual put on its best face and drew the strangers in with gently smiling jaws at the prospect of so much profit – all those people had to eat and drink, many would crowd into the little shops around the Clock Tower and buy souvenirs of Ferrycarrig Regatta, many single people would get so drunk that they would stay the night – a useful little bonus at the end of the season. Over the whole day would hover the fragile happiness of summer almost gone, a last fling before the bright lodges would be locked and shuttered for the winter, the guest houses narrowed down to accommodate the odd commercial or so and the hotels reduced from summer employment of hundreds to the immediate family of the owners with one or two permanent helps.

Even in the rain it was always a cheerful day. People would resign themselves to getting so wet that it didn't much matter if the rain went on falling, which it often did, hut usually it was warm rain that did little harm to those it drenched. Competitors on the Greasy Pole would get wet anyway. Many of those were traditionally big men in navy blue suits, who might go around wet all day until they steamed dry in the pubs at night.

This Regatta however began with pearly skies and the ghost of a full moon going down behind the lighthouse. Yellow light before the sun came up filled the sky like melting honey and even at six o'clock in the morning it was warm. Why was I awake? Why was Ruth? She had never ceased being an early riser since the boys were infants, demanding food at dawn. I've always been a rather spasmodic early-morning enthusiast. If I'm awake I go and sniff the new day (sometimes even in Dublin) wondering then why I don't do it always.

The Ferrycarrig coastline of course is particularly beautiful, islands and inlets absorbing the light like petals, fragile-looking and impermanent. You blink an eye and when you look again something has changed. You go on looking long enough and the colours melt into one another as in a sloppy paintbox and, again, come clear and glowing in the strengthening sun.

I suppose I can remember that Regatta morning clearly because Ruth and I went swimming together and saw the earliest boats coming in and heard their hooters waking up the sleepy town. People came down to the water's edge to wave. Children from the docks area raised a cheer. You couldn't help feeling happy that the whole day lay untouched before us. On our way in to breakfast we dropped in on Eleanor who was already awake and by the window, wearing a summer dress instead of a nightdress. Somebody, probably Hanny, had obviously been in to wash her and brush her hair and prepare her for another day. Only this was not quite another day. Eleanor's summer dress proved it, and her air of waiting as for a theatre curtain to go up. We chatted to her about the lovely morning, about the Dingle boatmen who had already arrived, about whether or not we should arrange with the Mayor to present prizes right outside her window instead of on a rostrum by the harbour opposite. Eleanor had something resembling a smile in the dark undamaged eyes. She was not tense. I felt suddenly that even if I and Ruth had stayed with her all day she wouldn't have minded, might even have welcomed it. She conveyed to me that she would like the chaise longue moved to a slightly different angle in front of the window and I did that. She wrote 'Thanks love' on the pad and on our way out we met Hanny coming in with a breakfast tray.

Down in the kitchen Con was dishing up sausages which had been cooked with bacon and the local delicacy known as drisheens. In Eleanor's time in the kitchen he wouldn't have been allowed such a vulgarity, but Ruth and I and Andrew and Julia, not to speak of my happy mother and the boys, sat cheerfully down to the sort of breakfast the family seldom had except on Sundays but traditionally partook of on Regatta Day. As they told one another, you never knew when you might be able to snatch another bite, so eat up everybody. Con had the air of a successful chef. He dished and served the simple fare with a flourish, he made jokes and he flicked the tea towel, delighted to be feeding people who valued his efforts. Hanny had gone out to see how a sick neighbour was before the crowds made it impossible, and her absence was of course partly responsible for the festive air. Putting myself in Con's place, I realised how difficult it is to serve a meal with style and cheerfulness if one of your party regards you with suspicion and contempt. Hanny anyhow tended to feed her cats and herself early in the morning, to their mutual satisfaction.

The rest of us lingered over breakfast, vaguely plotting Regatta Day. For some reason, most of us liked to get as far away from the house as possible even although many of the main events would finish right across from the front door. The theory was that if you were too near the house, friends from further away up the coast might expect open house all day. The O'Donohues never minded this in the evening, indeed the house would be traditionally overflowing after six o'clock, but at midday a picnic up near the estuary was considered advisable. There was a vantage point out there anyhow from which you could see the whole harbour in perspective and the regatta scene reminded me of nothing so much as one of those crowded Venetian canvases of Canaletto. There was evidence everywhere of superb boatmanship; one of the things which never failed to fascinate me was the skill with which small boys and old men managed their little craft, nosing in and out through the bigger boats to make their way half a mile away to pick up a friend or relation. Ferrycarrig, you see, knew boats from its cradle. There was no important building in the town except the ruined Abbey that had not something to do with boats and their comings and goings over the centuries.

Eventually on that day none of us can ever forget, Hanny decided to stay around the house as usual – after many spurious deliberations – to keep an eye on Eleanor and her mother and (as we all knew) to take advantage of every scrap of gossip the visitors might bring to town. Hanny, on this one marvellous day of the year, would renew acquaintance with old school friends and others scattered along the coast but no unwelcome person would dare put a foot across the threshold.

Hanny and her few cronies would most likely spend the hottest hours of the day closeted in the kitchen and only emerge for the prize giving. Eleanor had already intimated that none of the cronies was to be allowed near her.

The rest of us packed the car in leisurely fashion with the makings of a picnic, with swimming togs, fishing gear and toy boats, with all the rest of the paraphernalia for a day out.

My mother came with us, so did Con and his children, but that was the year I bought the station wagon so there was room for all. We drove out of the excited town as soon as we'd watched a few preliminary competitions and out along the arm of the harbour that curved back towards the river. When we stopped as usual to look back, heat shimmered like fireflies above the town and the tide was a blaze of little boats. This was the time when it was good to get away from the midday crowds and not return until it was time for the main boat races of the afternoon. In fact I drove back much earlier, leaving the family scattered at ease after their picnic, because one of the boys had burst into tears when it was discovered that his was the only rod we had forgotten. I volunteered to go back for it because young Maurice believed that this was the day and this the place where he would catch the biggest trout of his life. So far he had caught nothing larger than minnows and sprats, but I went back anyhow, remembering what it felt like to be his age and knowing I could chat to Eleanor at the same time.

I'd never taken for granted her instant response to my arrival, the way she lit up every time. I looked forward to making her undamaged eyes laugh as I pushed in her door. Eleanor was on the couch where we'd left her all right, but fallen forwards on her face like a thin rag doll, bent double across her rug. When I gently prised her backwards I felt her still warm between my hands, but I had seen death once before and you don't mistake it next time. I judged she must have died, fastidious Eleanor, by inhaling vomit.

Her writing pad had dropped to the carpet and on it was scrawled her last undefeated piece of defiance. 'Who says I must wait until He calls?' On the ledge beside the couch was a smashed glass pill bottle. Tonight the fireworks would go flaring up past her window, and I had the odd feeling she would be watching, wherever she was. For everybody's sake I scrumpled up the piece of paper and put it in my pocket. It was a cowardly betrayal of Eleanor, but there were living people to be sheltered.

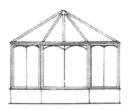

I like mornings. I like being awake and not awake. I like watching patterns on the ceiling and imagining that I can change them. Harbour light in Ferrycarrig is best, and lace curtains. At home we don't have lace curtains, just heavily lined ones even in the bedrooms. You get all sorts of stars and spangles on the ceiling in Ferrycarrig. I often lie far longer than I ought to, watching them, wishing the day would somehow melt into tomorrow morning and all you would know of it would be the changing of light patterns. In summer the light in Ferrycarrig is maybe a little like Greece, only not so clear. Sealight. Shadows of birds.

When I was a child I never saw my mother except in the distance. Sometimes I would play with her dresses. She had so many. Once Katina played with them too –

they fitted her better. Katina was tall and her hair was black like her eyes. She was too young to be my nurse but she helped her mother, Clea. That day we were playing with a ball on the terrace and my mother's windows were open. We stepped through white blowing curtains and into a room I had never seen before. The floor was pink marble and cool. The ceiling was very high, with birds and fruit and flowers at the corners. The door of an armoire was not quite closed and Katina opened it a little more. So many dresses, in so many colours. Katina asked me to get a chair and I carried it over. It was a small gilt chair with a cane seat. Katina stood on it and we heard a little crack as the cane broke, but not completely. Katina put her hand to her lip and we waited without moving.

The room door was slightly open but nobody heard. Nobody came. We heard the servants chattering in the kitchen. We heard Constantin whistling below the terrace as he weeded a bed of flowers. Katina lifted down two dresses, a gold one for her and a deep blue one for me. I was too frightened to put mine on but Katina put on hers over her own frock and walked like a queen across the floor, the gold hem trailing behind her.

She laughed and came back to dress me up too in a gown which was lace and smelled of flowers. But it didn't fit me, it was like wearing a length of cloth, not like Katina's. She held out her hand and said, 'Parakolo', pretending to ask me to dance, but then we heard footsteps. Katina said we must hide in the dressing-room – you got to it through a little white door in the far corner, but before we reached it somebody could be heard outside and Katina lifted me first into the wardrobe and stepped in after me, pulling the door almost closed. It was smothery and perfumed inside, strange but nice. It felt safe. Through the crack I saw Clea come in and put a vase of roses on Mother's side table, then look around the room with a surprised stare. Then she made an angry sound and crossed to the wardrobe quickly in her flat Greek sandals which flapped noisily on the floor. She had seen the misplaced chair and a fold of Katina's gold dress which had remained outside, and she pulled us out of the armoire very very angrily. Katina was smacked before Clea got Mother's dress back over her head and I was told I should be ashamed to allow Katina to do such things. How could I stop Katina doing anything?

When I was older I sometimes went to Mother's room alone after I had heard the door of the car bang at the time when they went out to parties on those evenings when they were not entertaining here. I remember the singing of cicadas as I tried on strange and lovely dresses. And I remember shadows, always shadows. I never put on the light. Reflections from the sky and the distant sea gave enough light for me to see myself in the long mirror which had flying golden cherubs at the top. I thought I looked nice. I thought if only I were allowed such dresses I would be different. I was never caught again. I got to know Mother through her dresses. Pure silk dresses light as feathers which hardly whispered as you lifted them down. Creamy Irish linen, much heavier. Others with white crochet lace collars and cuffs made by my grandmother. They came in little boxes from Ireland.

One of the maids sewed them on to black or dark red wool dresses for winter. They were always removed for washing every time she wore them, always sewn back on again by one of the servants. There was a crochet lace shawl too made by my grandmother which (Katina told me) Greek women found very strange and beautiful. At one stage Mother's little evening shoes, many dozens of them, fitted me too, and I would walk carefully about in them on the pink marble floor, slightly afraid of falling and damaging a dress. I never did.

Strangely, when I was in Mother's company I made all sorts of mistakes. My hands would tremble and I would drop things, knock over vases, generally make a fool of myself. I don't wonder she was reluctant to take me visiting. A diplomat's daughter ought to be able to move about without danger to her surroundings. I wasn't.

Mother, I think, was never consciously unkind. I irritated her, which was understandable. She only had to look at me and I felt unsure of myself, ready for the next mistake to prove her right. Had I been different she probably would have enjoyed taking me around. I know my father would have been pleased if I accompanied them, but he didn't know me at my worst. In his company I always felt easier. I had more confidence. He wasn't expecting the worst of me, which my mother had reason to do. I want to stress that it was no fault of hers. It was my fault. Even that business of the goldfish. I must have been eight. It was, I think, the year we left Athens.

It was my eighth birthday and I had had a party arranged for me that afternoon. Now it was over. Even Katina had gone home. All I had left of my birthday was a heap of presents, all of which I had looked at. Mother and Father were going out, naturally, but I knew he would come up to see me before he left. My nursery was at the top of the Embassy. From it I could see the Parthenon. I liked to watch the sunset behind it, always red as blood in summer. My father came into the room and caught my shoulders from behind.

'You're growing up, young Julia. No time before you'll be coming out with us. Maybe six years more.'

'I don't really want to go out to parties, Daddy.'

'That's because the time hasn't come. You will

when you are bigger and I buy you armfuls of gorgeous dresses like your mother's. Won't that be great?'

He kissed me goodbye as Clea stood respectfully to one side, and then to my astonishment Mother breezed into the room, beautiful as a calendar lady. She wore the gold dress Katina had tried on and her hair curled in a great mass around her face. She was smiling and kind, except to my father.

'Not that waistcoat, Con,' she said sharply. 'The one I had them leave out for you. Be quick and change or we'll be late.'

He kissed me and went, since he never argued with her. She knelt down kindly beside me. So tall she looked always in her evening dresses. So beautiful.

'I have an un-birthday present for you tomorrow, baby,' she said. 'You can look forward to it. Goodnight and many happy returns once again.' She hugged me and her perfume stayed on my clothes for a long time. I heard her satin slippers tapping down the stairs. I heard the door of the car banging and Nicolas driving them off through the Embassy gates. Clea helped me undress. I was very tired.

'Do you know what Mother has for me tomorrow?' I asked her.

'No, my lamb, but it will be nice. Go to sleep now.'

'Sing to me, Clea.'

Clea came from the islands and she had a rough yet

sweet and comforting voice. I didn't know what most of the words meant but I knew they were about the countryside and young goats being born on the hillside in early Spring and little flowers pushing up for them to eat. There was a lot of blood in the sky still over the Parthenon but I was asleep before Clea's song ended. I dreamed of little goats on the side of a mountain. I expected Mother would come to see me very early in the morning. This was something she had never done before.

Next day my lessons were over and lunch had been eaten in the day nursery and still my mother had not come. I was sure she had forgotten but I didn't want to go out walking with Clea in case I might be mistaken. Clea told me she had gone out already but she had not forgotten me after all. A big glass bowl was sent up from the kitchen, covered in a blue cloth. A servant left it on my table and went smiling away and I called Clea from the sewing room.

'Come and see me open it,' I said.

Clea came with pins between her teeth, carrying a half-cut-out bright cotton dress she was making for Katina. She always wore black herself, summer and winter. She shook her head and laughed when I asked her if she knew what was under the cloth and she said there was one good way to find out. I said I would like to wait for my mother but Clea said Madame would be very busy entertaining here at home this evening.

'Let us see, you and I,' Clea said, and her fingers reached for the blue cloth at the same time as mine did. We both laughed then. Underneath the cloth was a goldfish bowl of a partly clouded blue glass and inside were three goldfish as bright as the sun, swimming around very fast and seeming to bump their small black noses against the sides of the bowl. They were my best present. I could never tire of looking at them. I asked Clea about feeding them and she said Madame had given her the food – see! She would explain to me about changing the water in the bowl every week and help me, but I could feed them myself.

Now? Yes, now – didn't they look hungry? There was a little metal button in the box of ants' eggs with a hole through which you shook a little food three times, one shake each for the goldfish. I watched as the little glittering fish each rose to the surface and gobbled at the food, his eyes widening as he gobbled. I told Clea I would like always to feed them myself and Clea said, 'Bien sur.' Sometimes she spoke to me in French. She was trying to learn a little French from Mother. When she laid aside her sewing and said we were going for a walk I didn't want to go because of the goldfish but Clea said we would meet Katina on her way home from school and bring her back to see my pets. This was nice because nothing is any good unless you have somebody to show it to.

Katina was very excited. She said the fish were obviously hungry again and she must feed them this time but her mother spoke to her very fast in Greek so that I couldn't understand. Katina was cross for the rest of the afternoon, but Clea told me there are two ways of accidentally killing goldfish. One is by suffocating them in dirty water. The other is by overfeeding them. Finally Katina and I knelt up on the window seat and watched them flashing about in their blue bowl on the window sill, happy as we were, I think.

I wished Mother would come and see them so I kept sending her messages by Clea. It was about three weeks later when she walked in one morning, happy and in a hurry but ready to see the goldfish being fed. They seemed to be even brighter than when I had got them, and one had certainly grown bigger. I pointed this out to her as I went to fetch the food and she agreed. There was no reason why I should have felt anxious as I often did when Mother was impatient or angry on the occasions when I saw her. But my hand holding the small drum of fishfood was not steady – I knew this even before the awful thing happened. I shook the container too hard and even dinted it slightly against the rim of the bowl. The whole lid suddenly came off and an avalanche of food descended on the unfortunate creatures, covering all the surface of the water and clouding it below.

Mother slapped me furiously on both hands before grabbing up the bowl and making for the bathroom, but Clea bent to comfort me before she went to help. I simply cried and went on crying, drenching my handkerchief, my dress, unable to believe what had happened. Were the goldfish dead? And if they were, had I killed them?

The goldfish were not dead, but I think they began to die from that day. They no longer came and bumped their small black noses against the sides of the bowl when it was time to feed them. In fact they cowered together among the stones at the bottom waiting for the skies to fall in on them again. They seemed to me to lose their glitter day by day and eventually their skins became slimy and they grew sluggish, hardly moving. One morning when I got up they simply weren't there. Clea told me they died during the night and she had disinfected the bowl very carefully. We would get new goldfish in a week or two when the bowl had become a healthy place again. The bowl stood on the window ledge in the sunshine, water glinted in the coral arches through which my fish liked to swim, but word came up from downstairs that there were to be no more goldfish. I had hundreds of drachmae in my money box but there were to be no more goldfish. I tried pleading with my father who came up to see me most days, but he said some things were better left alone. He never liked to go against her – this I knew.

Once again, who was to blame if not I? I had been told how to care for the goldfish. It was surely easy. Yet I had made a mess of it and right before my mother's eyes. Why should she ever trust me again? I taught myself to forget the pretty flashing creatures in the sun, and I put their bowl away in a dark corner of the schoolroom. Next time I saw Mother she was friendly and brought me a honeycomb she had been given by country people in the mountains. Clea and I ate it Greek style in a bowl with bitter creamy yogurt.

It was after Easter by this time and we were beginning to talk about going home to Ireland when Athens became too hot in July. Clea would go back to her island and take Katina to her grandparents while we were away. Whenever I saw my mother she would mention Ireland and Grandmother and aunts Hanny and Margaret and my cousins. Sometimes she came upstairs with a letter and let me add 'Love from Julia'. What did it mean to me, going 'home to Ireland'? I was I think a little confused because home was here. Home was my toys and Katina and Clea's hugging at night and her strange harsh songs that I loved to hear. I knew I was Irish but I didn't know what being Irish was.

At home in Ireland I felt anxious all the time. Ferrycarrig was beautiful and it was never too hot, but after the first day of hugging and kissing and welcoming home things changed very quickly. Sometimes in the evening sitting in the drawing-room with Aunt Hanny, Aunt Margaret and my mother, I thought I could feel their dislike of me. They often spoke in the first person plural when they meant me. They said things like 'We have neither grace nor charm', and 'the thing is, of course, we are not very intelligent', and I honestly believe they weren't aware I could understand. I may not have been very intelligent but I wasn't an imbecile. Even my father's attitude changed towards me when we were at home in Ireland. Always kind in Athens, he tended to become abstracted in the old house as though he too had to work very hard and keep on thinking up new ways to stay abreast of things. It was during these holidays that I learned my mother and he often quarrelled, or rather she often quarrelled with him. If they did this abroad, I never knew of it. We occupied not only different parts of the official residence but different worlds as well. And servants – which the family in Ireland did not have at this time – absorb a great deal of friction between members of the same family.

Sometimes I can remember wakening up in Ireland and looking out across the harbour from the tiny windows of my attic room (Mother's room when she was a girl) and wondering how the day would pass until I could be safe back between these four walls again. I wasn't allowed to read or sit in my room during the day because it was considered 'unhealthy'. I had to dismantle my bed every morning and hang the sheets up to air, then remake the bed every evening before getting into it.

The pleasant happenings of the day in Athens – dancing lessons as well as those in the schoolroom, music lessons, walks with Clea, swimming lessons and visits to the Museum, or maybe just playing with the cats in the kitchen garden – were replaced by tasks to keep me busy. I had to dust and tidy my parents' room every morning and help Aunt Hanny in the kitchen. I could go swimming only when these tasks were finished. My mother explained that living a rather artificial life abroad with servants always at hand must not be allowed to render me unable to take care of myself – and others.

The person I feared most at this time was my grandmother. At least once a day I had to visit her – take her the post, a drink of milk, or merely see that she was all right. She was usually sewing in her upright chair by the window and she always greeted me the same way.

'Who are you, child? Stand up straight and don't stammer.'

'I'm Julia, Grandmother. Aunt Hanny says would you like a glass of milk?'

'She knows perfectly well I never touch milk at this time of day. What did you say your name was? Don't fidget, and pull up your socks.'

'Julia, Grandmother.'

'Whose Julia are you? Is Alex your father?'

'No, Grandmother. Con is.'

'You mean Eleanor is your mother? Now I understand. Tell Eleanor I wish to speak to her and then go at once to your lessons.'

'Yes, Grandmother.'

Every day she thought I was somebody else, but at least she had no way of finding out whether or not I did lessons. I would reduce the weird interview with her to two simple instructions to myself: tell Hanny no milk and tell Mother to go to her. This second instruction sometimes got me into trouble. At Ferrycarrig my mother often became indolent, even dreamy. I would find her on some rainy morning among a heap of old dance cards or photographs or schoolgirl diaries in the back drawing-room, curled up happily like a girl of sixteen, hating to be disturbed. I think perhaps the pace of the life she lived in Athens made it essential for her to slow down while she was here. She would look up genuinely startled, a pencil caught between her teeth, ready to smile until she saw who it was.

Sometimes when I came upon her like this, simply dressed in her old clothes and even a bit tousled, I realised how beautiful she was, how different from other women. The summer I was twelve I remember coming upon her like this and being about to say, 'Show

me, and tell me what it was like when you were young,'
but I quickly choked the words back when I saw the
familiar impatience on her face, the exasperation that
here once again coming to get in the way was her ugly
and boring daughter who should have been a son. Aunt
Hanny told me once that when I was born, only boys'
names had been thought of for me.

I think it was the following summer we adopted
Andrew. I remember being delighted at first at the
prospect of having a brother and then being worried in
case my status would sink lower still in my mother's
eyes.

I needn't have worried. Andrew did not find favour.
He was shy and plain and red-haired and burdened
with a strong English accent when he first came to live
with us in Cork. He was so often jeered at and unhappy
in school that sometimes he didn't attend at all but went
off mitching for the day – not with friends, because like
me he had none, but always by himself. Sometimes I
would go looking for him after school and bring him a
banana or a bun I'd salvaged from my own lunch. He
was often around the Lough, skimming stones along
the water, or kicking them, or just sitting and watching
people sail model boats. Sometimes if we stayed too
long on a fine Spring evening we both got into trouble
for coming home late. At other times my mother might
send Gobnait to look for us. She was our young cook-

housekeeper at that time, bad-tempered with us because she was given a hard life by my mother.

All this of course was during the war, when diplomatic relations were broken off all over Europe, and my mother had to be content with the dull life of a provincial town. We could have lived with my father of course – he worked in Dublin for the British Embassy in some supernumerary capacity or other and he had a flat in Fitzwilliam Square. But my mother rather strangely refused to live there, preferring to build up a practice in Cork and be nearer to Ferrycarrig.

Father came down most weekends, sometimes by the dreadful wartime trains if petrol was even harder to come by than usual, and sometimes she packed a beautiful dress and went back to Dublin with him to attend some function or other, leaving us with Gobnait. During these times I believe I got to know Andrew quite well, the Andrew who hid behind a mulish face when Mother was present to judge him and find him lacking.

He told me something extraordinary once. We were sitting together on a stone bench near the Lough one late afternoon in April when the warmth was just beginning to go out of the day. Most of the children who had been sailing boats had gone home. We knew we should have been at home ourselves. But Andrew sat swinging his scratched legs and chuckling while the long shadows gathered all around us.

'He made me a boat once,' Andrew said, 'I wish I had it now.'

'Who did?'

'Dad. But I hardly ever sailed it.'

'Why?'

Andrew shrugged, then chuckled again. 'He was too fond of it himself. Kept telling me I wasn't sailing it properly and he'd have to show me how. He was right too, I often capsized her. He could manage her like a real captain. Sail her in and out of the other boats on the Round Pond and always keep her on course. Once when I came home from school there was a note from him on the table saying he'd taken the boat to the Park to try her on a new tack and he'd wait for me there. He was on leave at the time – it was wartime. When I got to the Park there he was surrounded by kids and showing off how good he was. He didn't even see me for half an hour. The Janet we called her. Mother's name. He wrote it in red along her bows.'

'Did your mother ever come sailing her with you?'

'She was nursing at the time. Sometimes if she had a day off she came to the Park. She had some Sundays off, but they always stayed in bed late and put a note on the door saying, "Please don't disturb". You know,' Andrew said, grinning.

'Oh.' In fact I hardly knew what he was talking about at that time, although I was years older than he was.

'Different when I was a little kid,' Andrew went on. 'Then I just went to their room soon as I wakened up and got into bed with them.'

'You got into your parents' bed with them?' The idea was so extraordinary that I could hardly believe him. 'They didn't mind?'

'Course not. They'd roll over and make room. Put me between them if I was cold. Sometimes I'd fall asleep again and wake up not knowing where I was. Then we'd all have a good laugh.'

It was very cold by the Lough now, and we both got up to go home. But although I was going to my real mother, I was no more eager to arrive than Andrew was, whose real mother was dead. Sometimes of course when my father was at home he'd come to meet us on the way and if he did he was always kind. He'd warn us if Mother was cross and he'd advise us to apologise first, and not to argue with her. Andrew became a different person as we neared home. He would stop chattering, his walk would slow down. By the time we were at the gate his face would be stubborn again, like a house with closed shutters. And he would look plainer than anybody could believe possible who had seen the leg-swinging cheerful red-haired boy down at the Lough. When eventually Andrew was sent away to school I missed him. He told me however that he loved school and hated the holidays.

It was the opposite with me, but then I didn't, as they say, do well at school. I was hopeless at games in a convent where all the most favoured girls were on the camogie team or good at athletics. When I played camogie I was always afraid of being hit by the ball or having my glasses broken by the camogie sticks. I had no skill or dash or courage and when teams were being chosen I was always picked last and was a sore trial to the captain. Eventually they allowed me to opt out and study during the games period, but I don't remember ever doing much work. The voices coming up from the playing fields distracted me. Down there everybody was friendly with everybody else, everybody belonged there. I didn't really belong anywhere and I had no friends now that Andrew had gone away.

I don't think it would have made any difference even if I had been encouraged to bring girls home with me to the house. Probably nobody would have wanted to come, but the other girls in my class did go quite often to one another's homes for tea or even to study together. I didn't even know how you got on terms like that with anybody. When I made a remark among any group in my own class, people tended to look at one another and smile, not so much at what I said, I think, as at the idea of my having an opinion about anything. I always ended up sorry I had spoken, and I usually ended up walking off by myself. Music lessons were some consolation. I was not bad at music, but not good enough to be remarkable in that school where several talents were the norm. In my final year the Games Captain, for instance, won a gold medal at the Feis Ceoil in the soprano solo class and nobody thought it strange except me. I was glad to do my Leaving Cert at last and gain enough marks to take up a course in Veterinary Surgery in University College, Dublin. I'd always wanted to be a vet since I first learned it was possible to earn one's living looking after animals. I begged my father to let me go to Dublin instead of studying in Cork, and he pleaded my cause with Mother even though by this time he had given up the Dublin flat and retired to Cork.

Dublin was strange but I liked it – a place where you could get lost and not be criticised. I stayed in a house in Terenure in those days when it was still possible to find lodgings and the family was friendly, especially the son Tony who was a year ahead of me in College. Whenever I see the word friendship written in a book, I think of Tony Costelloe. He was red-cheeked and curly haired and he spent a lot of time playing snooker. I liked him because he was the first boy I ever knew who didn't think me odd. He would issue invitations like, 'Why don't we go to the pictures?' or 'Come down to Rathmines and I'll show you how to play snooker,' and his casualness made me forget that nobody had ever issued invitations like that to me before. In the beginning I looked for reasons. Had his mother (a kind Corkwoman always busy in the kitchen) asked him to be nice to the new girl from home? Did he treat every new student in his parents' house with the same compulsory friendliness? Certainly I never saw him putting down anybody but as the year wore on I stopped looking for reasons why he should be kind to me. He became that extraordinary thing, a friend of mine, and he asked my opinion about things like which sort of shoes he should buy or what books he should read.

We cycled down to college together in the mornings and in the spring we joined An Oige and went hostelling at weekends. Tony was great at getting a fire going with damp logs in some little place like Glencree or Glenmalure and he could knock a meal together out of bits and scraps that tasted good after a long hungry cycle across mountain roads, maybe in the rain.

When I was with him I wasn't afraid of other people and I stopped feeling I was different. I enjoyed being one of a group for the first time in my life, and when I went home at Easter my parents were astonished and pleased. Andrew, who was home too, told me I looked almost pretty – what had happened? I had just stopped being afraid of people, that was all. I thought I would never be afraid of anybody again.

I went back to Dublin delighted at the prospect of the summer term and even eager to prove myself at the

Pre-Med. I was stupidly confident. But almost from the beginning things were different. I have always hated being touched by anybody, even being bumped against by people in the street. I feel threatened and panic-stricken when it happens, even if they themselves are not aware of it. Tony, when we were walking or cycling together, had never, so to speak, crowded me. I had never got the feeling that I'd have to edge closer to the wall or to the kerb to escape contact. I'd never thought about it at all. Early on in the new term this changed. He sometimes put his arm around my shoulder, very casually, but I hated the weight of it and wanted to get away. When I did move out of reach he looked surprised and hurt, and once, in the country, when we were cycling over Calary Bog he attempted to loop an arm around me to push me up a hill and I got off the bike at once and walked along beside it. He cycled on up the hill himself and waited for me, but he looked offended and baffled, for the first time. I felt shy of him, and wished I were safe at home. Much later on that evening he questioned me, and after that I never felt the same about him again.

'Do you,' he said awkwardly, 'prefer the company of girls?'

At the time I didn't even know what he meant so I remained silent, and at last he apologised and left me alone. He was busy with exams anyway, and so was I. But I had already decided I was not going back to his house again next term. Ever since that day I'd felt trapped.

In fact, I did so badly in my exams that I asked my father to let me give up the attempt to become a vet and train instead for children's nursing. He was surprised and my mother was contemptuous, but they found me a place in Fairy Hill and I was happy enough for a while. The work was hard, especially for trainee nurses, but I didn't mind that. One day towards the end of my first year I was told there was a visitor for me in the hall, and there to my astonishment was Tony Costelloe, smiling as though I had only seen him yesterday. He asked me when was my day off, and I agreed to meet him on Thursday at the Metropole. We went upstairs for tea and later we took a bus to Dalkey where we walked around for a while. It was early summer, and I'd forgotten how pretty Dalkey was. I kept wondering why he had come to see me after all this time and finally, sitting on a bollard in Coliemore Harbour, he told me. He was going to be twenty-one at the end of May and he wanted to invite me to his party which would be in a little hotel here in Dalkey. He'd take me there so that I'd know where I was going, and not be anxious.

'I don't like parties of any kind,' I told him unhappily, 'you know that.'

'Come on, you'll like mine, Julia. I dropped in to see you because I specially wanted you to come.'

'I'm no good at parties,' I said, 'I can't talk to people and I'm always sorry I didn't stay at home.'

'It won't be like that,' Tony assured me. He was about to put a hand on mine when he obviously remembered Calary Bog and drew back. He clasped both his hands together and looked smiling down at them. 'Please come, Julia.'

'All right,' I said.

That was the first and last twenty-first birthday party I was ever at. I don't want to talk about it or even remember it. It's so long ago anyway. I did see Tony once more. I was with my father on our way to attend a specialist in Dublin. By then Tony was a qualified vet and married, but he ran up to us in the street like a young boy and insisted that I introduce him to my father, who asked him to meet us afterwards in the Shelbourne for a drink.

It was then I learned that Tony Costelloe was the father of a two-year-old son. He and his wife Pauline took the child cycling into the mountains every weekend, perched on a special little seat fitted to the back of his bike. Pauline always cycled behind to keep an eye on him. No, he never used his car except for work, Tony said. He invited both of us back home with him to meet the family but we had to get the train back to Cork. I promised to phone him next time I was in Dublin but I never did.

What followed when I abandoned the nursing course and came home is all like a dream now. I gave up menstruating and one day seemed to melt into another, one season into another, without noticeable change. I often forgot what month it was, but not, of course, June. That was the month we packed up a good deal of our belongings and migrated as always to Ferrycarrig, there to live over again all the summers of childhood – that's what I did, at any rate. It was as if I actually became a child again in my parents' eyes as soon as I stopped pursuing a life of my own, and I can't complain about this. I felt safe at home and the price of safety was what I suppose you could call a kind of servitude. My mother, not my father, exacted this, and really she cannot be blamed. As a young girl herself she had fought her way into a profession where very few women had practised before her, and she had done well even after her marriage. In those days marriage was accepted as the end of a career, but she worked in a sort of way even in Greece and Egypt wherever her services were needed, and later set up a fairly large practice in Cork. When she came back to Ferrycarrig, as she did every year, it was as a respected member of the family, not a failure.

My case was different. I simply gave up. People frightened me. In particular relationships terrified me. My reaction was that of a snail who retreats back into his shell at a touch. When the shell made its annual removal back to Ferrycarrig, that was all right. I was simply picked up and moved with the rest of the family's belongings. There was nothing to be afraid of except my mother, and on holiday she was less frightening than at home. The worst times were the early days when she thought she could direct me into some other occupation. She would occasionally bring home bundles of leaflets or a career guidance book or forms for me to sign. I signed whatever she wished but I seldom posted anything. The bushes around the Lough contain various failed plans of my mother's to find a career for me. The odd time I did go for some interview or other, but since on such occasions my tongue used to stick to the roof of my mouth making it impossible to articulate a single word, I was in no danger of being selected for anything. Once my father spoke to a friend of his about a secretarial job for me and I did a shorthand-typing course for two weeks out of an eight-week session, but after that my parents obviously decided that my future was with them and they must make the best of it.

I felt like a small animal sheltering from a storm and suddenly finding it was over, and the sun was shining again. Housework ceased to bother me since it was the price of staying at home, and I had the pleasure of feeding an army of stray cats in the back garden. For my twenty-third birthday my father bought me a pair of goldfish in a superbly beautiful bowl, an act of such kindness and reconciliation that it took my breath away. Every summer after that we packed the fish up and brought them to Ferrycarrig. They flourished for five years and finally died of old age, to be replaced by another pair. My father said nobody had ever kept goldfish alive so long. My mother smiled, but quite kindly. For long periods we got on well together. She often gave me beautiful old dresses of hers for the summer holidays. I seldom had new clothes but that was because I expect my parents knew how embarrassing it was for me to try on new garments and be laughed at by shop assistants. I never mind being ignored but I hate being laughed at.

When my cousin Martin married Ruth, I had friends every summer. Like Tony long ago, they never gave me the feeling I was odd or unlike other people. To them I was a person worth talking to and spending time with as an equal – although to write this down makes me laugh. But it's true. There were times when we went for picnics across the Ferry and I completely forgot myself in their company and that of their children. There were long lazy afternoons when it was good to be alive, to feel the sun and swim with them in a brimming tide and lie about afterwards lazily talking or playing with the children. Mother liked them too and never minded my being with them. Father, like myself, became different in their company. They were people pretty close to my age who, incredibly, took happiness for granted, who expected everything to be simple and manageable, and it was. Once only with Ruth was I disturbed by something I saw, but that was on the evening of the day my mother died which was a terrible day anyway. The children had been put to bed and Ruth had gone up to tuck them in. I had gone up for the same reason myself and there, through the half-open door, I saw my father on his knees in the children's room, his arms around Ruth's body, his head held sideways against it as though listening for a pulse. There was such an expression of concentrated pity on Ruth's face that I doubted if she were ever aware of the oddness of his posture. Anyhow neither of them saw me and I went quickly away, slightly sickened to see them together like that and rather frightened too.

Later, downstairs, Ruth was perfectly normal, pouring drinks and making tea for all the neighbours who came in, she and Martin coping as you would expect with the shocked weeping of Hanny and Margaret. I didn't see my father for the rest of the evening. I think he may have been drunk. But next day he had recovered. He was very pale but kind and attentive to Andrew and me even though he was busy arranging every detail of the funeral.

There was a solemn Requiem Mass for my mother in the parish church which the county council and all the town dignitories attended in ceremonial robes – I presume this was because of my grandfather's position.

There were so many wreaths of flowers that a special little room was set aside for them, and a special trailer carried them behind the hearse on the way to the cemetery. Once in Egypt I saw a film of Hamlet and the fair Ophelia's grave was arranged like my mother's. It was entirely lined with grasses and flowers, and it had ropes of pink wild flowers from the clifftops hanging down into the earth from the four corners. I was told later that my father decided on this and had gathered the flowers himself. Nothing like it had ever been seen in the town before, that was certain, since by custom flowers arrived only with the coffin and were spread over the filled-in grave. But there against the wall of the ruined Abbey (older, of course than the town itself) was this brilliant grave beside my grandfather's headstone, and I well remember the gasp of the mourners when they saw the wild flowers and the ropes of purple and white ribbons to which they were attached. There was even a little uneasiness, as though some unwritten law of the Church were being broken by having the opened-up grave decorated so flamboyantly.

I heard the whisper of one townswoman to another on the way out. 'Would you doubt Eleanor O'Donohoe would have even her grave done up like a maypole?' she said in her friend's ear, but I heard her anyway, and I smiled because probably my mother would have liked the theatrical gesture – or rather she would have liked it if she didn't know it was my father's idea. Maybe now, wherever she is, she understands him at last. She had thought enough of him once, after all, to marry him.

He stood very straight and handsome and soldierly during the last prayers when most other people's heads were bowed. I looked at him for courage and held on tightly to Andrew's hand as the Parish Priest prayed. 'To you O God in Sion, to you must vows be fulfilled in Jerusalem. Hear my prayer: to you all flesh must come. Eternal rest grant unto them, O Lord, and let perpetual light shine upon them . . . Be merciful, we beseech you, Lord, to the soul of your handmaid Eleanor.'

He was an old man, the Parish Priest, and he repeated over the coffin some of the traditional prayers we had heard already at Mass. Earlier the phrase 'your handmaid Eleanor' had not really impinged. Now in the breezy sunshine of the old graveyard I thought it so strangely inappropriate that I couldn't help smiling. Catching myself, I lowered my head and covered my face with one hand. Ruth's arm came around my waist and I had to wriggle it away. I felt trapped and strange and closer to my mother than I had ever felt in her lifetime.

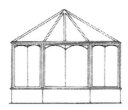

It was little Pappy knew all those years ago when he left me a life interest in the house that I'd see the lot of them down and be laughing here after them. 'Hanny,' he used to say, 'when your Mother and I are gone they'll not elbow you out, because you'll be mistress of this house so long as you're alive, and after that let them fight it out between them.' 'Twas funny none of them ever minded talking as if I already had one foot in the grave because in the beginning it was true. I was thought to be the shakings of the bag, the lame calf they'd never rear because I got every disease known and unknown to man and I a young one. When I was born Mama was too old, they thought, to have a proper healthy child – in fact 'the shakings of the bag' was probably the first mysterious grown up phrase I ever puzzled over. Mama gave the lie to them all when Eleanor arrived two years later, her masterpiece you might say, the flower of the flock.

Being weak and sickly wasn't such a bad thing, looking back. I never really felt sick after the pneumonia cleared up and I was finished with scarlet fever, mumps and measles. What I did feel was pleased at all the petting and cosseting, pleased that nobody was ever allowed to lay a finger on me whatever I did. If anything like butter or eggs or cream ever went short, I was the one to get the last of them. When jobs were being doled out, I had only to give a little cough and I was excused. Pappy took me driving with him in the trap whenever he went visiting in the country, and until I was ten I had lessons at home from Mr Hogan.

A child reared at home is always listening. I knew things nobody else knew. I knew why visiting aunts and neighbours lowered their voices even before Mama put a finger on her lip up in the drawing-room and asked me to fetch something for her from the kitchen. On the way down I always waited for a while and listened outside the door. I knew why certain girls in the town had to be sent to Dublin and I knew why the likes of Con and his raft of brothers and sisters had no father. I knew who was coming to stay in the house before anybody else did and I knew about illness and coming births and deaths in the family when nobody else had a whisper of them.

'Did you ever in your life see such a knowing little

face as Hanny's?' people used to say, and knowing it must have been, because I knew everything. But I always bided my time before telling it. Most times indeed I kept quiet. If I'd made a nuisance of myself, caused trouble too often, my fine times might all be at an end, and well I knew it.

Fine times they were. To this day I can still feel the first spring sunshine on my face when Pappy would have Mama dress me up to take me with him into the country. Maybe he would have business in some little town like Rosscarbery and he'd take the opportunity to call to see my grandmother in his old home.

'Hanny, is it?' she'd say, holding my face in her hands because her sight was almost gone. 'Nobody but Hanny could have the like of this little doll's face. Leave her with me, let you, for the day and be off about your business until it's time for your dinner. You'll take it with us, Maurice?'

'I will to be sure, Mother,' Pappy would say, giving a touch of the whip to the pony and rattling off along the dusty road. Maybe that day I'd find the first open daffodils beside the stream that ran through Grandma's farm and maybe I'd see a hare sitting up tall on his haunches, paws hanging, ears up, looking around in all directions before racing like the wind around a field. Wild as a March hare. It wasn't a line from a lesson book – I knew what it meant, all right, and Grandma told me

153

even more. 'That fellow you saw is looking for a wife, Hanny,' she said. 'He knows she's watching just out of sight and he's showing her his paces before asking her.'

One day my tall half-stupid uncle Matt (one of the two unmarried brothers left on the farm) brought in a hare for the pot hanging by its four tied feet and I cried so much that Matt was told to take him away out of that and give him to the McCarthys for their dinner. We'd do with eggs for today. I followed Uncle Matt out and stroked the dead hare's bloodied fur that was as soft as a cat's and I asked him not to shoot any more hares. He went off grumbling and I ate eggs for dinner that day although I hate them. I kept seeing the wide-open frightened dead eyes of the hare for a long time after that. In the summer, in late May or early June before the others got their holidays, it was even better. I would be free to roam the fields of buttercups and daisies and devil's bread-and-cheese and huge red poppies and ox-eye daisies, free to dangle my feet in the stream and listen to the skylarks or go gathering honeycombs with my grandmother from her four blue hives sitting among lavender bushes and golden furze at the bottom of the flower garden. The singing of bees when you lift the lid of a hive is a sound I've remembered all my life, the sound of summer and plenty, of a strange life going on down there before your eyes, with rules of its own that have nothing to do with our rules. Bees and summer meadows and hot feet cooling in a stream of golden pebbles and long days of idleness were my lot when the rest of the family had heads bent over examination papers, clothes sticky against their skin in the stifling classrooms. I used to think of them and hug myself with triumph. The weak shall inherit the earth, not the strong. And when my father's business would be over I'd have as well the long cool drive home in the evening, lime trees dropping scented blossoms above our heads, rooks circling the fields for the last time, the ghost of a moon coming up over our town while the sun sank lower in pure gold over the clock tower. Who would want to be strong and healthy? Mama would be at the railings watching for us to drive up the Mall under the trees and there would be exclamations of delight from everybody as we unpacked the newlaid eggs and the honeycombs, the farm bread and the flitch of smoked bacon. We were given a great welcome after what had been for me a day of pure self-indulgence and delight.

Childhood never seemed to end. My brothers went away to school and my sisters too for a couple of years but I stayed on at home, suffering one further bout of rheumatic fever which merely secured me in my invalidhood and meant that all I'd ever have to do would be help sew on name tabs for school clothes to be packed into the tin trunks. It was a particular pleasure for me – since everything I did I did neatly and with care – to pack the folded clothes between tissues into the big trunks which were lined with cream green-striped linen and had the name Cash's of Cork on the inside of the lid. I could print neatly too and I would turn out identical pairs of labels (one for each side of the trunk) which read MASTER ALEX O'DONOHOE PASSENGER TO FERMOY VIA CORK, OR MISS MARGARET O'DONOHOE PASSENGER TO DUBLIN. That was as near as I ever wanted to be to going away. When Pappy's eyes got bad and he refused to wear spectacles, I would often be asked to read out the letters that came back home every week. One of them is before me as I write. Spidery handwriting, you must imagine, and several blots from tears. At that time I was the only one able to read Alex's handwriting.

My dear Mam and Pappy,

Thanks for your letter which came today. We are settled in to work now after two days back at school. I got a B today for Maths and was excused games because of a cold. Maurice is well and says he will write tomorrow. The dormitory is very cold. Some fellows keep their socks on. I forgot my blue fountain pen, Pappy. Could you post it on and if you don't mind send me some Cleeve's toffee and a packet of fig rolls, also a mapping pen and some more of Mam's jam and my autograph album which I forgot. Love to Hanny and all at home from

Your loving son, Alex

Alex was greedy and never wrote a letter without asking for something, even if he'd gone away with a mountain of food in his box. I wouldn't bother reading out requests for Cleeve's toffee or jam if I knew he didn't need them. I'd just mention the pens and the autograph album, and Pappy would post them the same day. I knew anyhow that if the priest who checked the little boys' letters home had been able to read Alex's awful writing, he would have returned the letter and told Alex to rewrite it leaving out references to extra tuck and his cold. The boarders were not supposed to tell news which might worry their parents so you normally only heard about illness after the boy was better. Of course a cold wasn't so serious, but even so I was sorry I had read it out because Mama started to worry about it and (I well remember) sent on an extra wool rug to Alex. The trouble with Alex's letters was that if you left out what he wasn't supposed to write, you were left with precious little, and anyhow very soon after this Mama sent him a headline book and his writing improved to such an extent that everybody could read his letters. It was out of my hands then and they could waste their time if they liked making up parcels of tuck which Alex mightn't even get if he was in punishment, which he often was.

My own school, when I eventually got to it, was around the corner and up the hill near the lighthouse, so near to the house that they allowed me home for dinner. I liked this because only very few girls were allowed the privilege – delicate ones like me. The boarders used to give us money to bring them back sweets or jam rolls or bottles of fizzy lemonade but usually I refused because it was against the rules. I would do it for one girl when I was struck on her – being struck was carrying around a photograph of somebody and dreaming of her at night and swearing you would die for her if necessary. The nuns forbade such pairs of girls to sit together in class or share the same dormitory. There were Children of Mary with blue ribbons in every class to spy on the others and report them. In time I became a Child of Mary which I was glad about because nobody spied on us.

School was a place where I learned little I didn't know already except a bit of French and how to avoid being caught. It was essential to be a good liar and look truthful – both I could do with ease. Being small and delicate was of great assistance. A fit of coughing occurring at the right time made people pity you and could be useful on occasions, but never when Eleanor was at home.

Eleanor – I suppose we were rivals right from the day of her birth. I had been the small miracle, the living proof that a miserably weak premature baby didn't have to die if everybody took enough care. Then came Eleanor when Mama was two years older. From the moment the midwife looked down at her and said she'd be a beauty, people have gathered around Eleanor as the most natural thing in the world. She was pretty too, of course, and cleverer than anybody else. 'She's foxing,' Eleanor would say to Mama about me when I had established my right to stay at home from school because of a headache, 'look at her eyes!'

Eleanor even as a small child didn't care about people but everybody liked her. She had huge brown eyes that often made speech unnecessary. She could run like the wind without getting tired and at school she was the best in the class at Maths, the best at English and French, the wing who scored all the goals at camogie, the girl chosen to present bouquets to visiting Big Wigs and read addresses of welcome. Since afterwards she could do funny imitations of how the important visitors talked and walked, the girls liked her too. People didn't notice me when Eleanor was in the room. One of the two beaux I ever had – that was when I was twenty – met Eleanor one time she was home from London and never looked at me again. If he called afterwards it was only to be given news of

Eleanor who didn't even remember his name the next time she came home.

I well remember when Aggie Donovan came back with the news that Eleanor had a black beau in London – well, not exactly black, but what was the difference? Aggie said he was from Ceylon and already a qualified doctor at twenty-four years of age. Mama nearly had a heart attack and Pappy was going to go over to London to bring Eleanor home. Bring her home! Little he knew Eleanor. It was I who told them to take things easy and maybe it might blow over. Eleanor never stayed interested in anybody for long. But Mama of course had to enlist the help of Con and look where that led. Right up to the day of the wedding I thought Eleanor would call it off – she'd so often laughed with me at the airs and graces of Con O'Riordan.

Con never changed much for all his airs and graces. I've seen the same goat's gaze turned on young Ruth that he used to give me and Eleanor and even Margaret long ago. Greedy like a goat and watching his chance to get you on your own. What kept him from making any declaration of any sort to me was the way he could see I was sneering at him (without saying anything) because of the way he was dragged up. He lived in Tinpot out there beyond the paupers' end of town. I remember him when he hadn't a boot to his foot, trailing along to school in tatters with his feet covered in dust or even in mud if it rained. He was always whistling. A little while later, at the boys' school and he still without boots, he always seemed to be marching behind a brass band that nobody else could see, showing you he didn't care about being fatherless, to all intents and purposes, and ragged and without prospects – or so anybody might think.

Of course he wasn't without prospects – not Con O'Riordan. Cunning like all his tribe, he had the future mapped out for himself if only he could get the County Scholarship and go away to school. Nobody thought he would, not with the disadvantages of life in Tinpot. But I said he was cunning, and that he was. He made up to the headmaster with his smiling airs and he got extra lessons after the rest of them went home. He'd often be there until six o'clock with no doubt the poor Master falling out of his standing with the hunger. Con was reared like a goat and I don't believe he ever suffered long from hunger or anything else for that matter. He'd take what was going here or anywhere else and he'd sing for his supper by way of a story or a joke or a lot of old guff of some sort that amused people who didn't know any better. Mama used to pity him and keep him to tea if he came helping in the garden. There was nothing he couldn't do in the way of jobs, and you may be sure he framed the first halfpenny he ever earned. When the scholarship came his way at last he was in the position of adding to it and buying all the clothes he needed to go away to school. At boarding school in Cork he took on the ways of a gentleman, but he never fooled me, the same Con. In time to come he even fooled Mama, but I could cut him down to size any time with a single look, and well he knew it.

Heaven alone knows why Eleanor finally married him. Boredom, I suppose. The war was over and she could travel with Con to the far ends of the earth. Also she knew she could manage him, do whatever she wanted and still have him grateful she married him. Also he was handsome. I have to give him that. And full of fun, with stories always ready to tell you. I know because we were walking out for a short time – a very short time. He didn't like my sharp tongue and as I said I thought him above his station. People who lived at his end of town usually knew their place and kept to it: the kitchens, the dairy, the garden. Con, being clever, had as I said been educated above it, but that didn't give him the right to all those airs and graces. Mama liked him of course. She thought him handsome and very helpful – a nice civil boy, which he was. It was she who first thought of him as a safe husband for Eleanor – that was the rock he perished on! And deserved to, of course. There were girls who might have made him happy, maybe not so pretty or so clever as Eleanor, but girls who were good enough for him, had he only known it.

The night before the wedding Eleanor suddenly

realised what she was doing. I remember the evening very well, St John's Eve, and the flames of bonfires at all the front windows. There were three fine fires blazing in the Mall, shooting up sparks into the dusk that fell back into a full tide. There were a few stars but no moon.

When we had everything ready and the wedding breakfast set out in the dining-room with all the best silver, I suggested putting out the lights so that we could see the bonfires better. The girls who came in to help us had gone home, or gone to dance around the fires more likely, and Eleanor had grown very quiet. For half an hour Mama had been urging her to take a warm bath and go to bed, but Eleanor stayed around the house, picking things up and leaving them down, going to the window and being lit by the flames, sitting down and getting up again. I brought Mama in to see a splendid bonfire the Corcorans had got going at the very end of the Mall, and Eleanor suddenly threw her arms around Mama and burst out laughing.

'You're all going to get the shock of your lives tomorrow,' she said, 'because I'm not marrying him. I was mad to think of it.'

'This is no time for jokes, Eleanor,' Mama said. 'You should get to bed now as soon as possible like a good girl.'

'You're not listening to me. I've changed my mind.

Marry Con the Shaughraun? The thing is crazy. All this must have happened before – people male and female must have changed their minds at the last moment.'

'The husband-to-be in Great Expectations did, Eleanor,' I said, 'Remember Miss Havisham wouldn't have the table touched and left the flowers to moulder away with the wedding cake for years? I think if you've changed your mind it's just as well you did it in time. Do you want me to go around and tell Con?'

'You, Miss, will go straight to your bed this minute,' Mama said sternly. 'Call Pappy on your way and ask him to come up here. And light the lamps before you go, please.'

I lit the oil lamps, turned up the wicks slowly, and saw the whiteness of Eleanor's face under the springy mass of hair that we'd have a job fixing a veil on tomorrow. A hundred hairpins were laid out in readiness up in her room. Before I left them, Eleanor was in tears and Mama had poured out two small glasses of port wine.

'Be quick and fetch Pappy,' Mama said sharply to me and off I went, wondering about all the wedding presents displayed in the drawing-room and indeed all over the house – would they all have to be sent back? Who would tell everybody so that they wouldn't appear all dressed up in the Parish Church at eleven o'clock? The wedding was off and I thought it just as well. Con O'Riordan was not going to be my brother-in-law after all.

When I told Pappy why he was being called he stroked his chin and said, 'Aye, aye – it's an anxious time for a young girl. She's not the first bride to lose her nerve and she'll not be the last. I'll go and speak to the child.'

'But Pappy, she's made up her mind. She's not marrying Con tomorrow after all. I know Eleanor when she means a thing.'

'Go to bed, mouse,' Pappy said kindly. 'Everything will be all right. And don't mention this little upset to anybody. Eleanor will be laughing over it tomorrow.'

Of course Eleanor was. She was laughing at any rate, beautiful as the youngest sister in a fairy tale, with little roses pinned around the train of her dress, and Grandmother's creamy veil of Limerick lace held by a wreath of orange blossom as well as one of the hundred pins. I remember the blackness of her eyes under the veil and all the aunts and uncles exclaiming over the beauty of her and the handsome groom who matched her in all but breeding. His straggle of poor relations sat at one end of the table slightly awed as well they might be, and held their knives as though they were pens and mumbled little jokes to one another. His mother called my father 'Sir' and knocked over a glass of champagne which two maids rushed to mop up. Alex poured her another glass which is more than I would have done.

165

Con himself was bold as you please, white teeth glittering at his own jokes, making the perfect bridegroom's speech which he had probably learned by heart from some etiquette book. Everybody laughed and raised their glasses to the happy couple and Eleanor threw her bouquet to Margaret before she went upstairs to change and Margaret was married to another stupid man before the year was out.

She threw her bouquet to me, but I had more sense than the pair of them put together.

Margaret's husband was a schoolmaster who couldn't teach, though he fancied himself very good about the house and was always poking into everything. He had a nice pair of dark eyes like a whipped spaniel's which he passed on to young Martin who, thank God, resembles him in nothing else. Margaret had to fend for James and her children just the same as if she wasn't married, and I wouldn't mind but she thought the world of him. When they'd all be home here in the summer it was Con who felt the lash of his wife's tongue, not sleepy James.

The day I finally knew Eleanor regretted getting married was the day I saw her grimace and wipe her mouth after Con had kissed her goodbye. He had to go on business to Dublin and she refused to go. I was standing at the pantry door and I saw the two of them between the curtains in the hall.

'You might enjoy the trip, love,' Con was saying, but Eleanor shook her head.

'I don't want to breathe in the smoke and fumes of Dublin when I might be lying on the rocks here in Ferrycarrig. Goodbye, Con.'

'I'll see you, love, on Wednesday then,' Con said, kissing her before he went out the door, and then I saw the look on Eleanor's face and her instinctive gesture when he had gone. Some marriage! I could imagine how she must have regarded the rest of it if she couldn't even bear a kiss on the mouth in broad daylight from him. Lips wiped clean, she came whistling down to the kitchen to me.

'Snooping as usual, Hanny?' she said. 'Let's go for a swim before anybody else is up.'

'Some people have work to do,' I said. 'We can't all be like you.'

'Anyway I prefer my own company,' Eleanor said, 'the quality is more consistent.'

'What about the baby, Eleanor?' I reminded her. 'Won't she be awake soon?'

'Margaret will see to her with her own lot,' Eleanor said carelessly. 'I'll take them all off somewhere later. Oh Hanny, I'm so bored that I think I'd even welcome a fatal illness for the sheer drama of it!'

'God between us and all harm! Stop it, Eleanor, and you with everything most women could wish for. That's wicked talk, and well you know it.'

'I only say things like that to shock your timid little soul, Hanny. Don't pay any attention. You'll only encourage me to go on. Tooraloo.'

She grabbed a blazer and a towel and strode off in the opposite direction to Con, the same free stride she had as a girl who had never known opposition. When I told Margaret later what Eleanor said, she blessed herself.

'It's all those foreign places where she's lived that have her ruined,' Margaret said, 'We must be patient and let her come to her senses these holidays. Did she take Julia with her?'

'She seemed to think you'd see to Julia.'

'So I will,' Margaret said easily. 'One child extra is no bother to wash and dress. James will give me a hand.'

Imagine a man helping to wash and dress young children! You wouldn't believe the silly face of him and the way he coaxed them and made jokes just the same as a mother would. I heard him and I passing the landing. He and Margaret had them all spruce and down to breakfast in not much more than half an hour, by which time Eleanor strolled in with wet hair after her swim, all the cussedness gone out of her and a sweet smile on her face. True to her word, she took all the children off to the far strand later, and kept them happy for the rest of the morning while Margaret and I got through the baking and preparation for lunch.

Those times we had only a woman in from Con's end of the town every morning to clean the house and polish the brasses for us – gone already were the days when you could get girls from the cottages for five shillings a week with no nonsense about insurance or holidays or anything else.

Mama was already getting a little odd by the late nineteen-twenties. Poor Pappy was dead but she could never remember. She'd send messages to him and call Margaret's children by our names and talk about finishing some piece of lace or crochet before morning. That same lace was the finish of her, maybe. She was the star pupil and never lost her touch. The nuns persuaded her to keep at it, and bought all her stuff for a pittance. She often sat up all night over a lace collar that would be put on a green tweed cushion in the window of a craft shop in Dawson Street in Dublin and sold for a fortune to an American visitor. That never worried her, but all the close work at night affected her eyes and even her brain a little, I think. Certainly Mama could seldom concentrate on anything you said for more than a few seconds and then she would get all sorts of wrong impressions from inventing the end of your story.

She didn't like young Julia right from the beginning and she didn't like Margaret's James. She always called him 'that man' and sent him messages through Margaret or me. In fact you could say that Mam didn't like anybody who threatened to change the family in any way. She knew she had to accept husbands and wives if she wanted her children to come back to her, but apart from Con she never liked any of them. She liked him because he flattered her and was good-looking. Also she felt responsible for that wedding which was so nearly called off. She sometimes listened for hours on end to Con's old guff and laughed at it. I often heard her praising him to Eleanor who used to shrug and walk away.

Where did they go, those years that it seemed would last for ever? I enjoyed them as much as anybody. I saw babies grow into toddlers, into schoolchildren, into students, into husbands and wives and eventually into parents. There used to be four birthdays here from June to September – Eleanor's, Margaret's, Julia's and Martin's. I used to bake cakes for them all and Con would never forget to buy the candles. The summer Eleanor was forty (although she looked thirty) was the year they adopted Andrew. The adoption papers came through with her birthday cards and she tossed them impatiently aside. Con picked the papers up, put them in his pocket, and went to find Andrew.

'He's ours now,' Con said happily, leading him back down into the kitchen. 'Congratulate us on this auspicious day.'

Margaret ran forward and hugged Andrew who as usual stood like a white calf at a fair, looking doubtfully from one to the other of us with his pink eyes, blinking. His mother wasn't long dead at the time. We all managed somehow to kiss him and congratulate his new parents but I pitied them. He wasn't only a stupid boy and not even good-looking at that, but his mother was no better than she ought to be – not, of course, that this was the child's fault. It hardly fitted him to join the family, however. I remember he went over to Eleanor and took a small wrapped parcel from his pocket.

'Happy birthday, Aunt Eleanor,' he said quietly, showing that he hadn't even the wit to call her Mother. Eleanor thanked him but didn't open the parcel. Young Martin, who was seventeen or eighteen then, asked if he and Andrew could go out fishing if they promised to be back in time for the birthday lunch, and he put an arm on Andrew's shoulder as they went off together. A nice boy Margaret reared in Martin and he even had the wit to pick a nice enough wife in young Ruth when the time came. So many summers they all arrived and went away. I always connect bonfires up in the garden with the rattle of suitcases in the hall and the feeling that Mama and I (once Pappy was dead) had too much space to ourselves all the winter long in this house. We rattled around like peas in a box. We washed and put away the summer curtains, we sorted the china ware, made new cushion covers, bottled pears, framed the year's crop of First Communion or Confirmation or wedding photographs. We touched up bits of paintwork, made marmalade, and at the first blink of spring sunshine we got down the ceiling brushes and went cobwebbing. I say we, but naturally Mama did few of these jobs. I had to rely on the odd bit of help from the far end of town and somehow the winter passed and there were plants to be repotted, windows to clean, bedding plants to put down again in the garden and the chimneys to be swept by Runty O'Donovan. Mama never believed in the new vacuum brushes, so by the time Runty had climbed up and pulled down mountains of soot we had more cleaning and washing to do and the summer curtains to put up again. That would be at Easter and then the heavy winter curtains (which were not always washed) would be hung out in the sun to air before being folded away in camphor balls and stored in one of the oak blanket chests which had come with Mama from the old house in Kerry. She brought them to this town with her trousseau and two dozen handwoven wool blankets which we still have and two or three thick patchwork quilts which were old even then.

At Easter it would be time to think about the summer again, and anyhow Con and Eleanor and the children always came down for that weekend, indeed even during the years when they were abroad they sometimes got home for Easter bringing us strange sweetmeats like halva and honey cake and nougat with almonds and cherries. Eleanor and I would often talk about the old days when Mama would hide painted eggs up in the garden and we children would hunt for them before breakfast. That was before the days of chocolate Easter eggs. In cities, of course, children were sometimes given sugar eggs coloured and decorated, but we were quite content to vie with one another finding coloured real eggs to carry in to breakfast. You had to boil and eat as many as you found. Long ago it was not unusual for the father of a family to eat six eggs on Easter mornings and even more. Now that I eat hardly anything myself I find this difficult to believe. Food is a trouble and you often feel worse after eating than you would otherwise. I often throw up these days after a meal, so I've grown used to living on tea.

After Easter in the old days it was no time at all before examinations and the school holidays and then the house would be filling up again. So many summers. So many births. So many deaths.

Pappy had hardly settled for a few years into this house before a heart attack none of us ever expected carried him off. We waked him for two nights and got through three whole hams and a dozen chickens and several barrels of porter to feed the friends and neighbours who sat up all night with us. He had a funeral that was talked of for a long time afterwards, which was only right and proper since he was the County Manager.

After the burial Mama became stranger. She often sent him messages by one or the other of us as though she had forgotten he was dead and we grew used to encouraging her in the make believe world she had built up to hide in – all but Eleanor, that is. Eleanor called her bluff and believed it was better for her but Mama was stronger even than Eleanor. She stayed safe behind her own four walls, and outlived her son-in-law James and many of her children and even Eleanor herself.

James was a nobody, as I said, a weakling and a poor provider. When he and Margaret retired to this house you'd hardly know he was here. He had some wild idea of giving lessons in the town, making a show of himself in other words as though he were a young fellow, but it never came to anything. He became like one of those paper cut-out dolls you see little girls playing with. He and Margaret would go to the pictures one night a week and that was his big day. He would spend hours getting ready and dress himself up in his Sunday clothes, for a three minute walk around the corner and down the main street with Margaret linked to his arm. Several times they asked me to go along with them but I couldn't be bothered. He'd spend the rest of the week reading books in corners or doing little jobs around the house that nobody asked him to do, or he'd be down at the shops looking for ways to spend the money that was needed for other things. I often wondered why

Margaret didn't scream with the annoyance of him but she had great patience always and no doubt she'll get her reward for it. He was no catch for any girl, that's for sure.

One evening in late April he wasn't in the kitchen at tea time as usual and nobody knew where he was. When seven o'clock came and went and there was still no sign of James, we set out to look for him. The shock on Margaret's face is a thing I'll never forget when we found him at last sitting in a shelter above the lighthouse staring out at the sea, his face as white as chalk and his hands clenched.

The doctor said the cancer was far advanced and he didn't know why James had never complained of pains or anything else. He died after five or six weeks in the Cottage Hospital and Margaret sat with him for hours every day. When I went to see him he didn't know me but kept babbling about the isles of Greece and burning sapphires or what sounded very like it. He was a man who should never have taken on the responsibilities of a family when he couldn't cope with them.

Margaret took his death very hard although anybody would have thought she'd be glad to be free of him at last. She went up to stay with young Ruth and Martin in Dublin after the funeral and I believe she wouldn't put a foot outside the door, not even to go to the pictures, a thing she'd always liked. When she came back it was well into May and the weather here was lovely. I thought that would cheer her up. But she wouldn't budge outside the door all that summer except to sit maybe up in the garden in late July with an old photograph album collected when she and James were young and their children only babies. She wasn't much good in the house, but then Margaret never was, having gone off and she very young to train for a teacher.

In time she came to herself again – the first improvement was when Martin and Ruth came down in August with the twins and she couldn't very well refuse to go out across the ferry with them for picnics. She improved by degrees after that, but every Sunday saw her up at the grave, maybe for hours doing little bits of tidying or planting a great show of bulbs for the spring. That seemed to ease her a bit and I have to admit the grave was a credit to her the following Easter. She had cried so hard at the thought of a new grave for James that we let her put him in on top of Pappy and she had his name inscribed by Tim Power of Drumalong, and the date of his death. It just said 'James O'Connor, beloved husband of Margaret' and then the date. It went against the grain with me to let him into that grave at all but I didn't want to upset Margaret any further. However bad a mistake she made, he was the father of her children and I don't suppose we could have pushed him out in common decency to her. So there he lies under his shower of daffodils and tulips and little purple crocuses, and later primroses and begonias and Bachelor's Buttons and pinks and heather – she has plants for every season, and little dwarf conifers as well dotted over the wide resting place of the O'Donohoes and those that joined them in marriage. It was when we were burying James we discovered the remains of two little babies, baptised you may be sure but probably never christened and not mentioned on any tombstone. Families were large in those old days. I suppose the six of us should have been eight.

They're all down there now, young bones and old bones under the spring bulbs that have multiplied over the years. Those that loved one another are quiet together and those that couldn't stand the sight of one another quarrel no more. Eleanor and Con, for instance. They were a pair of opposites whose marriage had no chance at all, but I thought he'd lose his mind that Regatta day we found Eleanor. It was young Martin found her, of course. The bed was ruined but that didn't stop Con going down on his knees and trying to gather up Eleanor in his arms. We got him away at last, but Martin wouldn't let me wash her or change the bed before the doctor and the priest and the Guards arrived. They locked the door and Martin stayed a long time in there with the lot of them. Formalities like this are always a bother after a sudden death, I suppose. At last they let me in to wash Eleanor before Con carried her upstairs to be laid out. She didn't weigh much more than a child and when we had her eyes closed and her hands joined with Pappy's big crucifix between them, she looked the same as ever she looked only a bit paler. She looked tired too, as if she'd come on a long journey. But she also looked as if she might at any moment open the big eyes and tell you to go away until she called you. She may have been a wilful spoilt baby at the tail-end of a long family but I think Eleanor accepted her cross from God's hands the same way a saint might have done and she was no saint. It can't have been easy. She and Margaret got on better than she and I, but that was only natural. Sisters closer in age never agree. Eleanor and I fought over everything and over nothing but I always did my best for her when she became an invalid and I hope she knew.

It was strange that summer after Eleanor died. Con and Julia stayed on and often went walking together, a thing they never did before. I suppose they felt closer together because Eleanor had rejected both of them and Andrew (away in the Army) as well. She left everything she had to Martin and it amounted to twenty thousand pounds apart from her jewellery which she left to young Ruth. Martin divided the money equally between Con, Julia, Andrew and himself, because he said he wasn't entitled to it at all but didn't want to abuse Eleanor's memory by taking nothing.

How must it feel to be rejected in death by the person you have lived with all your life? I suppose I should know, being in the same position, in one way, but it was worse for Con. You'd never know it, the way he behaved. He never discussed that aspect of things at all, and he brushed it away if you referred to it, which I often did because I was curious to know what he really felt. I never did learn. He was as closed to the strange affair of Eleanor's Will as Mama was to her death. Mama simply continued to send messages downstairs to Eleanor, about being sure to eat enough, about being sure to take her pills, about coming up to see her as soon as she was feeling better. Eventually we left her happy in her delusions, and reported as she wished that Eleanor seemed a little better today and sent her love.

When eventually Mama died she was over 100, but she hadn't lived in this world for more than seventy of those years. She was still a handsome woman like Eleanor with a face that had no more lines on it than mine. What would age her, when she ignored what she found disagreeable? When she was dead we found mountains of fine handwork in her room, put away in boxes, folded in drawers, lying in neat piles on top of every surface covered by old linen pillowcases.

If the family lasts till the crack of doom it will never run out of lace tablecloths and table mats, tray cloths, lace-trimmed napkins and lace collars and cuffs that went out of fashion in 1935 and now (they tell me) are coming back. Some time I must sort them all out. Some time before that room collapses like the room below it in a cloudy heap of rubble in the orchard.

Con, if I allowed him, would have kept the house together, but who would be dependent on the likes of him?

Winters come and go, and I have moved down (now that Margaret too is dead) into the front room where Eleanor was found. Living down there makes it easier to keep warm, easier to get to the kitchen, easier to feed the cats, easier to open the door to the odd neighbour who calls, easier to see who's knocking if you don't want to let them in at all. Sometimes I hear the old house rattling around me on a winter's night and I think maybe the best thing that could happen to me would be if myself and the house were found dead in a heap together. Certainly I'll never move, never go to live with Con, or with Martin and Ruth as they have asked me, never give up my freedom to go into a home. Why should I? I'm content to take the consequences of living alone on little money, and whose business is it if not my own?

In a way I like it on my own. If Pappy could only know I'm the last of them all, I'm sure he'd chuckle the

180

way he often did when something amused him secretly. Life interest in the house indeed! They all died off one by one, and here inside the four walls are all the things they coveted and collected. Here in the rooms I never go to now are the old scrapbooks they gathered as children, the school trunks full of old letters and diaries, the photographs, the dance dresses, the combs and the button hooks, the christening shawl and the wedding veil that passed from the grandparents right through the family.

These things will go from them to their children and grandchildren, to young girls and boys that aren't dreamed or thought of yet. Young Martin often said he would always find his fishing rod next summer in the exact spot where he'd dropped it on the last morning of the holidays, and indeed I always took care that if something was taken away so that the floor could be cleaned, it was put back again in the self same spot. There's no cleaning done now – I wouldn't waste my time on it. I read and re-read the novels of Dickens, especially Great Expectations, and I play Patience – sometimes all day in winter. The odd person calls with a fresh loaf of bread or a few fresh eggs which I never eat, and there are times when I think I'd like to get out to the shops. But what for?

Even if I did eat real meals now, the house holds more than enough food in bottles and cans to last my time. We were always preparing for an army, Mama and I and then later Margaret and I. We would always say to one another, 'Remember the summer is on the way – we have to lay in stocks of food for a full house,' and so we did. So much, in fact, that it will never be used up. There's even sacks of flour and sugar stored in the old summerhouse in the corner of the kitchen, Alex's white elephant. We found it a good place to hide sacks that wouldn't look well standing around. It never shielded a single face from the sun, but, like everything else, we found a use for it. You only have to wait and you find a use for everything.

One of these spring days I'll take a walk upstairs and look at the rooms on the first landing and open up the windows in case Martin and Ruth come down to stay for the Regatta. Their boys are big now but they might come too. I never encouraged Con and Julia and Andrew after Eleanor died. They come to see me now and again but they always drive back home the same night. You wouldn't want Con to be meddling, poking his nose in here and there and telling you what must be done next if the house isn't to fall down. It will last my time, that's for sure. And later, let them fight it out as Pappy said. He wasn't thinking of those young people when he said it, but of the family. I bested the lot of them in the survival game. While they sweated it out at their examinations I played in summer meadows or paddled in my grandmother's stream. While they mated and married I made no fool of myself for anybody and I'll not do it now. Let them knock at the door and go on knocking before I'll listen again to advice I have no intention of taking. I'll go to no hospital and I'll submit to no tests. I've lived long enough to know what going for 'tests' means at my time of life. I'll have none of them, and if it means my only company will be the cats, what better company could anybody have? Cats offer friendship and even affection if you want it. If you don't, they leave you alone. I often think of all the cats that have shared our lives in this house since I was a child, white cats and black cats and tiger cats and ginger cats and every other coloured cat you could think of. 'Hanny's cats,' people always said, and I suppose they were. I it was that fed them. I feed them now when I don't bother feeding myself. They live better than they ever lived, in fact, because all the tins of cat food have been used up and I feed them tins of stewed steak from the larder – some of those tins must be twenty or more years old and it's time somebody opened them. Four of the cats that come creeping along the broken walls to me every day have no names and the rest are called Birdie, Tom, William and Bouncer. William is my real cat, as lovely a cat as you'd meet in a day's walk, a black cloud of a cat with eyes the colour of primroses and a coat as silky and soft as a hare's. His long fur blows this way and that in the breeze, and his little bones are light and brittle. He's seven years old but he still has a kitten's face. Even his paws are black and they feel like that silky leather the Italians used to make up into ladies' gloves fine enough to pack into walnut shells. He's the only cat I've ever allowed to sleep on my bed – that's because he's light as a feather and smells fresh and sweet as new leaves. He didn't thicken and grow fat like most castrated males. He didn't take to food, as most of them do. After the first shock of injury, he behaved as if nothing whatever had happened. He just started all over again his busy life of play and serious hunting.

He killed a rat three days afterwards, and in a week he was jumping walls again and climbing apple trees. I knew if I didn't have him castrated he'd never remain my cat. He'd go wandering off, get injured in fights and stay away for weeks on end. He might never come back at all. So I made the decision and never regretted it, until I realised he was sometimes a target for proper tomcats. He seemed to have lost his belligerent instinct towards them and sometimes he suffered for it. He asked for no pity. Once he had a badly infected cut above his eye which got worse and must have been painful. He stopped eating and one day he went away to die. Cats do that. You notice one day that old cats are not there at feeding time and when you search you find them hiding in some peaceful place, waiting like the stoics they are for death. I found William one morning almost indistinguishable from a heap of blackened leaves on top of the apple house in mild autumn sunshine and he wouldn't come when I called him, or give me his famous croak of welcome. I got a ladder and put him into a basket with a lid on it and then took him to the vet. An injection cured him and in a week he was as beautiful and lively as ever.

Most of the other cats kept to the yard, but William often chose to stay indoors, especially when I used to go out to the shops. He would be waiting with his croak of welcome behind the hall curtain when I came in. The house never felt empty. He would come with me into the kitchen, hop upon the table and inspect the messages. He didn't clamour for it at once if he smelled fish. He would go and sit in his usual shaft of sun by the door and purr loudly until he was called, the smile never leaving his small black face. Cats smile by looking at you and narrowing their eyes, then widening them again.

I haven't seen William for two days and I know why. He's had a swelling for some time now on his left back paw and he couldn't walk properly on it. He should have been taken to the vet weeks ago, but I don't go out any more. He has gone away somewhere to die and this morning I'll hunt for him. I'll get Mrs O'Donovan or the next person that knocks at the door to tell the vet to call but first William has to be found. I'll tell him he's a fool. At seven years of age he has half his life before him yet. Needlesqueak was fifteen when she died and then she blew out as easily as a candle. William will last my time and then Mrs O'Donovan will look after him for me. Let the rest of the cats take their chance. There's enough rats around the yard to last that lot for ever. They'll soon learn to hunt again. But I made a fool of William and when you do that to an animal you should stand by him. I'll go out there and find him this morning now that it's warm and soft again and nearly April. I might even get some seeds sown while I'm up there. It's growing weather and everything is beginning all over again.

Tara
press

188

CPSIA information can be obtained at www.ICGtesting.com
Printed in the USA
LVOW08s1930270616

494278LV00007B/690/P